KT-382-638

THE SHEIKH'S SECRET SON

Kasey Michaels

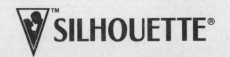
SILHOUETTE®

To Melissa Jeglinski, one more time.

*Silhouette and Colophon are registered trademarks of
Harlequin Books S.A., used under licence.*

*First published in Great Britain in 2001.
Silhouette Books, Eton House, 18-24 Paradise Road,
Richmond, Surrey TW9 1SR*

Special thanks and acknowledgement are given to Kasey Michaels
for her contribution to the FORTUNE'S HEIRS series.

© Harlequin Books S.A. 1999

ISBN 0 373 65036 1

117-0401

*Printed and bound in Spain
by Litografia Rosés S.A., Barcelona*

Fortune's Heirs

Meet the Fortunes—three new generations of a family with a legacy of wealth, influence and power!

Eden Fortune: The last thing she expected was a reunion with the father of her child. And she never anticipated that her feelings for the dashing and virile sheikh would be stronger than ever.

Sheikh Ben Ramir: He'd lost Eden due to his family's interference. But now the time had finally come for this lion of the desert to make his move and claim the only woman he'd ever loved—and the princely heir he'd never known.

Baby Taylor: The stunning revelation about his parentage had repercussions for the entire Fortune family, especially his foster parents—Matthew and Claudia.

Wyatt Grayhawk: The rugged lawman knew the prominent Fortune family had weathered its share of scandals, and he was determined to protect his friends at all costs.

KASEY MICHAELS

is a *New York Times* best-selling author of more than fifty books. In addition to writing for Silhouette Books®, she has long been known as one of the premier authors in romance. Ms Michaels has been honoured with the *Romantic Times Magazine* Career Achievement Award for Regency Historical novels, and is also a recipient of the Romance Writers of America RITA Award and several others. Her career has been the subject of a TV programme, 'A Better Way,' and she has appeared on the NBC *Today* show. Ms Michaels enjoys hearing from her readers, and you may write to her care of Silhouette Books.

Paternity Shocker!

DNA tests conclusively prove that Matthew Fortune, eldest son of Texas billionaire Ryan Fortune, is the biological father of a child whose identity has plagued and baffled a family, national law enforcement and the entire state of Texas. Time for a quick 'scandal' recap.

One year ago, Matthew and Claudia Fortune's million-dollar-darling Bryan was snatched by kidnappers demanding a jaw-dropping ransom. FBI agents recovered a baby with the distinctive crown-shaped birthmark identifying him as a Fortune—but the child *wasn't* Bryan. Matthew and Claudia agreed to care for little 'Taylor' until the mystery of his parentage was solved.

Even in the face of hard scientific evidence to the contrary, husband Matthew claims he's never strayed. Hmmm...Taylor is about one year old and the newlyweds tied the knot a little over *two* years ago... Matthew must be using the new *new* maths for those figures to add up!

And more titillating titbits from the Double Crown Ranch... *Royally* gorgeous hunk Sheikh Ben Ramir in the close company of legal eagle Eden Fortune. Sources say these two had a fast-'n-furious fling in Paris years ago. And Eden's son, Sawyer, is beginning to look like a prince-sized secret!

Fortune's Heirs is a marvellous new set of linked novels that feature the fabulously wealthy Fortune family—their lives, their loves, their dramas and their secrets!

Fortune's Heirs

June 2001
In the Arms of a Hero Beverly Barton
Wedlocked?! Pamela Toth

July 2001
Hired Bride Jackie Merritt
Marry in Haste... Karen Rose Smith

August 2001
The Expectant Secretary Leanna Wilson
Shotgun Vows Teresa Southwick

September 2001
To Love and Protect Her Margaret Watson

*Membership of the glamorous Fortune
family has its privileges...and its price!
But even the wealthy Fortunes can't buy
love—that comes naturally!*

KINGSTON FORTUNE (d)

1st marriage
PATIENCE TALBOT (d)

TEDDY§ m FIONA BRADLEY — MAX — 13. REED — BRODY — CHRISTOPHER — 14. BRODY — 15. MATILDA — 16. GRIFFIN

2nd marriage
SELENA HOBBS (d)

MIRANDA
m Lloyd Carter (D)

KANE   GABRIELLE

RYAN

1st marriage
JANINE LOCKHART (d)

12. ZANE

4. DALLAS
m
Sara Anderson

2. VANESSA*** 10. VICTORIA

MATTHEW
m
Claudia Beaumont
Bryan

2nd marriage
SOPHIA BARNES

CLINT LOCKHART
brother of
6. JACE LOCKHART

†ROSITA AND RUBEN PEREZ

Anita   Carmen   Frieda   3. CRUZ   4. MAGGIE
m
Craig Randall

Travis

CAMERON (d)
m MARY ELLEN LOCKHART

1. HOLDEN 5. LOGAN 7. EDEN

Sawyer*

LILY REDGROVE
m
Chester Cassidy (d)

11. COLE* 9. HANNAH   MARIA

James a.k.a. Taylor

TITLES:

1. MILLION DOLLAR MARRIAGE
2. THE BABY PURSUIT
3. FOR HER BABY'S SAKE
4. A WILLING WIFE
5. CORPORATE DADDY
6. SNOWBOUND CINDERELLA
7. THE SHEIKH'S SECRET SON
8. AN INNOCENT WOMAN
9. HERE COMES HIS BRIDE
10. IN THE ARMS OF A HERO
11. WEDLOCKED?!
12. HIRED BRIDE
13. MARRY IN HASTE....
14. THE EXPECTANT SECRETARY
15. SHOTGUN VOWS
16. TO LOVE AND PROTECT HER

*   Child of affair
d   Deceased
D   Divorced
m   Married
*** Twins
—   Affair
†   Loyal ranch staff
§   Kidnapped by maternal grandfather

One

The wedding had been beautiful. But then, weddings usually were beautiful, wonderful. Eden Fortune's brother Logan had been handsome and adorably nervous. Emily, his bride, had been lovely and serene. Together, Logan and Emily had taken their vows and become a family to Amanda Sue, Logan's no longer motherless daughter.

Happy endings were nice.

Not that Eden would know much about that.

The digital clock next to her bed blinked itself past midnight, and Eden knew she couldn't just lie there and watch as it passed one, then two... counting down the hours all the way to dawn.

Pushing back the soft down comforter, she slipped from the queen-size bed; a bed too large, too lonely. Too cold and empty.

Sliding her feet into her slippers, she brushed a thick lock of dark brown hair behind her left ear, pushed herself erect, and padded to the doorway, led by the light she always left on in the hallway in case her five-year-old son Sawyer woke during the night and she had to go to him.

He was quiet tonight, probably worn out from their long day. But, if he did wake, she knew she could calm his childish nightmares. She could sing him nonsense songs and hold his small body close and rock him back to sleep.

But she couldn't answer his questions.

Ciara Wilde had heard Sawyer ask the most unanswerable question tonight, at the small wedding reception held at the Fortune ranch after the ceremony. Ciara was a sweet girl, and Eden had been happy to hear that she and her uncle, Jace Lockhart, planned to be married. In fact, Eden had been offering Ciara her best wishes when Sawyer had asked the first question.

The boy's timing was impeccable.

"Mommy?" he'd asked, tugging at her skirt, looking up at her with those penetrating dark eyes of his, eyes that lived in her memory, in her dreams...and in her son. "Amanda Sue has a mommy and a daddy now, doesn't she?"

"Yes, darling," Eden had answered as her stomach knotted. She must have betrayed herself in her tone of voice, or in the quick flush of her cheeks, because Ciara had taken her hand, squeezed her fingers. "Uncle Logan and Aunt Emily are Amanda Sue's daddy and mommy now."

Sawyer's bottom lip had come forward in a pout. "That's not fair," he'd protested, glaring past Eden to where Logan was sitting in a chair on the front porch, rocking a sleepy Amanda Sue in his arms. "Why can *she* have both a mommy and a daddy when I can't?"

Eden had immediately knelt in front of her son, this five-year-old with questions and heartaches too big for his small body. "Sawyer, I—"

"Not fair! Not fair!" he'd shouted, pulling away from her, running off toward the stables.

Eden had continued to kneel in the dirt, stunned, watching Sawyer's straight, sturdy legs carry him away from her, and then flinched as Ciara's hand came to rest on her shoulder.

"Do you want me to go after him, Eden, talk to him?" Ciara had asked, offering her help, her friendship, her comfort.

"No, thank you, Ciara," Eden had said, returning to her feet slowly, like an old woman whose joints didn't always cooperate. "He'll be fine. He's probably going to visit with his pony for a while. Hercules is quite good at listening to Sawyer's problems, as long as the carrots hold out. He just needs some time alone, and then he'll be...fine. Really, he'll be fine..."

Eden had been right. Logan had brought Sawyer back to the house about a half hour later, and the boy had held his uncle's hand tightly as he apologized to her for running off without telling her where he was going. Then, as Eden watched, and as her brother had given Sawyer's hand a small squeeze, her son walked closer, his body stiff and straight, and motioned that she should bend so that he could kiss her cheek.

Always the gentleman, her son, once he was over his temper. Almost princely in his forgiveness of her for his own impolite actions.

Eden smiled now as she opened the door to Sawyer's room and a wedge of light from the hallway spilled into the room, exposing her son's outline on the bed. Tall for his age, old for his age. Straight and strong. Oddly formal for a child, with the manners of a much older child, with the sometimes autocratic ways of the man he'd never known.

And yet he was five years old. Only five years old.

Eden tiptoed into the room, stopped, and smiled again. Her big boy. Her great big, brave, wonderful boy. With his thumb stuck in his mouth and his teddy bear, Fred, clutched tight in one arm.

She bent and adjusted the covers over him, then pressed a kiss to her fingers before touching those same fingers to his cheek. He was her baby.

Her baby with the grown-up questions.

And she was his mother, the woman who didn't have any answers for him.

Eden Fortune had been born to just that. Fortune. There was wealth, yes, but she also had a more important fortune, that of her family. Eden's was a large family, the sort that swept you up, welcomed you in. Sometimes smothered you.

But she tried to not think about that anymore, about how she had run away when the love and concern had felt more like pity. She'd been young then, young and stupid. Young, and stupid, and pregnant. More than a little worried that, after vowing never to be like her father, she had acted with his same disregard for consequences.

Cameron Fortune was dead now, killed when speed, alcohol and poor judgment had combined to send his car racing out of control on his way back to the ranch from San Antonio, the nubile young woman tucked into the passenger seat dying as well. He'd always been irresponsible and she'd promised herself that, much as she'd loved her dad, she would never be anything like him.

But despite her vow, Sawyer was born...the consequence of an impetuous love, unprotected sex, and no thought at all about consequences.

But if Eden was her father's child, she was also her mother's daughter, and she had the same for-better-for-worse character that had kept Mary Ellen Fortune standing at her husband's shoulder, loving him no matter what.

Eden had made a mistake, but she had owned up to it in true Mary Ellen Fortune style. She'd packed herself up, straightened her spine, her resolve, and done what had to be done. She'd had her baby, kept her baby.

And she'd never regretted her decision.

Buying the house in San Antonio had been one of her best moves, as now she was close enough to the ranch to have the love and companionship of her family yet far enough away to maintain her independence. She had her brothers, Holden and Logan, she had her mother, and the entire Fortune menagerie of loving aunts and uncles and cousins.

And she had her career. Eden thanked the good Lord every night for her career. Her career as an international business lawyer filled her days. Sawyer filled her leisure hours.

Nothing filled her nights....

Eden was running late Monday morning, always a warning sign that the whole day would be one full of glitches and irritating minor problems—beginning with her pulling a hole in her last pair of panty hose. She'd had to run to the local convenience store to pick up a new pair. Worse, she'd come downstairs to learn that Sawyer had awakened with the sniffles, and even though Mrs. Betts had promised to watch him closely and call the doctor if he began to run a fever, Eden had been loathe to leave him.

Which was silly. Mrs. Betts was more than just a housekeeper. She was Eden's friend, and she loved Sawyer to pieces. He'd be fine, Eden knew that. He didn't need his mommy hovering over him, feeling his brow and handing him tissues. It had been Sawyer who had told her that, too, and not Mrs. Betts. What an independent little creature she was raising!

Pushing back her jacket sleeve as her high heels clicked against the marble floor of the tall office building, Eden checked her watch one more time, grimaced one more time, and headed for the bank of elevators.

Naturally, her gas gauge had somehow crept all the way to Empty when she hadn't been looking, further proving her theory that a day begun badly never goes well. The stop at the crowded gas station had taken precious minutes she hadn't had to spare.

Still fretting over the time lost at the gas station, she tapped one elegantly clad foot on the floor as the security guard checked for her name on the list in front of him.

She looked at her reflection in the golden doors of one of the elevators, quickly running a hand through her shoulder-length dark brown hair, squinting a little as she decided that she probably should have worn more blush with her dark blue suit, for her cheeks looked a little too pale.

"Oh, okay, here you are, Ms. Fortune," the security guard said after what seemed an eternity of time, pointing to one of the names on his list. "And here's your security pass. You can just pin it to your suit, okay?"

Eden nodded, took the pass. She had taken three quick steps toward the last elevator in the hallway before she stopped, turned, and walked back to the desk. She was wasting more time, she knew, but she just had to ask.

"Henry, I've been coming here for two years now. I know you, you know me. I know your wife packs you meatloaf sandwiches every Thursday, and you've met Sawyer a couple of times—enough times that you know he likes those cherry candies you keep in your pocket."

"Yes, ma'am."

Eden looked at him a moment, shook her head. "So," she asked, pointing to the badge she'd pinned to her jacket, "what's all this? The checking the list, the badge—those two goons standing in front of the elevator that goes to the twenty-sixth floor?"

Henry stole a quick look over his shoulder at the "goons," then motioned for Eden to step closer, as if he were about to tell her some state secret.

"It's this *guy*," he whispered conspiratorially. "I don't know who he is, see, but he shows up about an hour ago. Big black limousine. Bulletproof, I'm thinking, and with a car in front, another in back. All these guys come piling out of the two cars, come marching in here, demanding all sorts of stuff. I had to clear out the whole lobby before the guy steps so much as a foot out of the limo. And then I could barely see him for all the guys walking with him, speeding him into the elevator, whisking him upstairs. Tall, though. I could see the top of his head. He had one of those *things* on it, you know? One of those headpieces or what-you-want-to-call-its."

The guard leaned even closer to Eden and his voice dropped another notch. "You know what I think, missy? I think he must be some government type. And not *ours*, neither."

"Sounds intriguing, Henry," Eden said, trying to sound suitably impressed. She'd only been working in international law for two years, but she'd already seen her share of important people—those who really were and those who only thought they were. "And was he definitely going to the twenty-sixth floor?"

"Like you said, missy, you've been coming here for a while now," Henry said, standing straight once more and nervously beginning to shuffle the papers in front of him, as if he knew he'd said more than he should. "We both know that's the only elevator that goes all the way to the twenty-sixth floor."

Eden frowned, thanked Henry, and headed for the elevator once more, mentally reviewing the coming meeting in her head, mentally going over the names of those expected to attend the meeting.

There were all the usual suspects, of course. Her boss; her boss's boss. Three other lawyers on her level, each one assigned to a particular area of international law. Her area of expertise was international law as it pertained to oil and gas rights.

Today her firm was to represent a triad of American companies hoping to do business in the small oil-and-gas-rich Middle East kingdom of Kharmistan. Which, she supposed, explained all the heightened security and the big-shouldered, dour-faced men standing on either side of the elevator. They had reason to be a nervous bunch, Middle East tensions being what they were.

Eden had a bad moment at the elevator—fearing she was about to be frisked for the first time in her life—before the two big-shouldered "goons" finally let her pass, muttering to each other in their own language.

She kept her smile bright until the elevator doors closed in front of her, then grumbled something that sounded very much like "male chauvinist pigs," certain that the two had difficulty believing a woman could possibly have anything constructive to do with business. Now there was a prejudice that had no trouble crossing international borders!

She forgot the guards and watched the numbers light up one after the other as the elevator swiftly and silently whisked her to the twenty-sixth floor. One last check of her watch told her she had cut it fine, but would arrive on the dot of nine.

She gripped the handle of her attaché case tightly in both hands, holding it in front of her in an unconsciously defensive posture, took a deep breath, and exhaled slowly as the doors opened. Several men standing in the lobby of the penthouse office suite turned to look at her, then turned away again to resume their conversation.

Eden continued to stand in the elevator. She couldn't move. Her feet had rooted to the floor, her brain had gone on stun, robbing her of the ability to walk.

The elevator doors whispered closed again and she collapsed against the back wall, her hand pressed to her mouth as she told herself not to scream. Not to scream, not to faint, not to run...run...run. Run out of the building. Run to her car. Run to her house, where she would grab up her son and then run some more.

Run as far and as fast as she could.

Thankfully, sanity returned before anyone summoned the elevator back to the lobby, and she swallowed down hard and pushed the Door Open button so that she could leave the elevator and join the men who had probably already forgotten her.

He doesn't know, she told herself, repeating the words over and over like a mantra. *He doesn't know, he doesn't know. And what he doesn't know can't hurt me.*

Drawing on every resource at her command—her upbringing, her independent nature, her long years of taking care of herself—Eden willed her heart to slow. Willed her lips to smile. Willed herself to remember who she was, where she was, and why she was here.

She was here to explain international oil and gas law to her bosses, to her firm's clients, and to a Sheikh Barakah Karif Ramir of Kharmistan or his representative.

Which one was the tall guy wearing the headpiece Henry had talked about? The representative? Or the sheikh himself?

Did it matter?

Because she knew this man, if not his true name or position. She'd never forget him.

He was the self-assured gentleman standing smack in the middle of the reception area, holding court over those from her office and the clients her office represented.

He was the devastatingly handsome man she'd known almost six years ago in Paris.

He was the fickle, duplicitous man she'd known as Ben Ramsey...and she'd borne him a child. A boy child, with his same aristocratic features, his same dark eyes and hair, his same elegant posture, his same almost princely air of confidence.

Eden didn't feel much like humming a chorus of "It's a Small World After All."

Jim Morris broke away from the group before the elevator doors had closed, and for once Eden was happy to see the ambitious young lawyer. Jim looked worried, which made her even happier, as that meant he was probably going to grab her by the elbow and quickly drag her into another room so that he could tell her why the universe was about to explode here on the twenty-sixth floor.

"Trouble?" she asked almost eagerly as she kept her head down, carefully avoiding the eyes of the dozen or so men who probably wouldn't have given her a second look if her hair caught on fire.

"That depends, Eden," Jim said, hurriedly taking her arm—she'd almost offered it, she was that anxious to be rescued. "Come in here, okay? And tell me, please, *please* tell me that you know why in hell the sheikh felt the need to be here today?"

Eden tugged her elbow free of Jim's tight grip

and sat herself down in the nearest chair. It was more elegant than falling down.

Her stomach clenched into a tight ball, and she swayed slightly as a wave of panicked nausea hit her. Had she heard Jim right? Ben Ramsey was a sheikh? For crying out loud, Sawyer was the son of the Sheikh of Kharmistan? No. How could that be? Ludicrous. That was simply ludicrous.

Oh, God. Jim meant it. Now she knew. Ben was the sheikh. Sawyer was his son, the son Ben didn't know existed, thanks to his defection all those years ago in Paris.

How much danger was Sawyer in, now that she knew? If she was to tell Ben...

She cleared her throat, tried to focus on Jim Morris. "So he is the sheikh, then? Mr. Klinger said he might show up, but I thought—but then I hoped...well, never mind. What you're saying is that the guy in the headcloth—what *do* they call those things, anyway—is the sheikh himself, and not just his representative? What's the representative's name? Wait, I have it in my notes."

She set her attaché case on the desk in front of her and quickly unzipped it, then pulled out a thick manila folder and began paging through it. She always kept a "cast of characters" in her private notes, just so she could cram for the final exam that was the actual meeting with her firm's clients.

Mostly, however, she was stalling for time, time during which she hoped to put her shattered brain back together.

"Ah, here it is. Nadim. Yusuf Nadim. How could I have forgotten? He's the one we've all been dealing with the most, right? Man," she said, pressing a hand against her belly, "I've got to stop this, calm down." She put down her notes, looked up at Morris, knowing she must resemble a doe caught in headlights.

She began to pace, trying to burn off energy as an oil well burned off excess natural gas.

"Is he here, too, Jim? This Nadim guy? I only saw one of those headpieces—Lord, what *do* they call them? I feel like such an ugly American, calling them 'headpieces.' I know what a kimono is, Jim, I know what a kilt is—I even know the proper name for those shorts some Europeans wear on special occasions, although the name escapes me at the moment. So why don't I know what those headdresses are called? Laziness, that's what it is. Sheer laziness on my part. I should be ashamed of myself."

Jim rolled his eyes. "I don't think that's important right now, Eden. What's *important* is that this Nadim fellow is back at the hotel, sick from the flight or something, and that the sheikh is here on his own, and making one hell of a mess out of six months of our hard work. Why couldn't this Nadim guy just have postponed the meeting? Why do we have to have this big shot, know-nothing Sheikh of Ara-bee here to screw up the works?''

Pulling herself back from the inanity of trying to calm her badly jangled nerves by thinking about headpieces, Eden did her best to slip into her professional role. Jim wasn't exactly known for his social skills, and he had just crossed the line.

"One, Jim," she began firmly, "you're out of line. Two, you're still out of line. Unless you want to be that redneck 'y'all' lawyer from Texas, and I don't think you like insults any more than anyone else does. Third—how so? How is everything going wrong? Today's meeting should have been nothing more than a formality. All the bugs were worked out months ago.''

"Got you, Eden. That was stupid. I'm sorry." Morris raked a hand through his thinning hair, hair he wore three inches too long in the back in an effort to make the world believe he owned more of it. Eden noticed, withholding a grimace, that he'd had his hair permed since she'd seen him last. Talk about someone who could benefit from one of those head-dresses!

She mentally shook herself, once more tried to keep her mind on what was important. Tried to pretend her private world wasn't falling apart.

"All right, Jim. We'll forget it. Now, as I said,

we should be ready for some signing on the dotted line this morning, shouldn't we?"

"Yeah, you'd think so, wouldn't you. You thought so, I thought so, everybody in our firm thought so," Morris grumbled. "But it turns out the sheikh—this Ramir fellow—is a lawyer of some kind himself, educated at Yale, if you can believe that. A Yalie! He's got, like, a million questions. We need you, Harvard. Harvard always beats Yale, right?"

"What do you want me to do, Jim? Threaten to tackle him? Besides, I saw Klinger out there, right?" Eden protested, feeling the urge to bolt sliding over her again. This was too much. Too much information, too many memories, too many fears. They were all crowding in on her, bearing her down, crushing her.

She could barely think. "Surely Klinger can handle this. We're just here for decoration at this point, Jim, and you know that. As I said, a few comments, a lot of ego-kissing, some signing on the dotted line, and we're outta here."

"How interesting, Ms. Fortune. And who will be kissing my...ego?"

Eden closed her eyes, wishing the action could make her disappear. The way he'd disappeared so many years ago.

"Oh, God," she breathed almost soundlessly,

looking at Jim Morris, whose thin features had turned the color of putty. Then she squared her shoulders, turned around, and looked straight into Ben Ramsey's eyes. Into Sheikh Barakah Karif Ramir's dark, mocking eyes.

"I'm sorry, Your Highness," she said quickly. "As you can imagine, you weren't supposed to overhear my associate and me talking. I apologize."

Ben kept looking at her. Staring at her. Staring straight through her. With Sawyer's eyes, damn him.

"You may go now," he said rather imperiously. "Closing the door behind you as you leave—something you might have considered earlier."

Jim Morris knew he'd been the one addressed, even though the "Ramir fellow" was still looking at Eden. He didn't hesitate in escaping the small room. Rats deserting a sinking ship moved slower than he did as he left Eden alone to face the insulted Sheikh of Kharmistan.

Ben took two steps in Eden's direction.

She backed up an equal two paces, until she could feel the edge of the table against her hips. She placed her hands on either side of her, holding on to that edge, her posture definitely one of defense rather than offense.

Which was stupid. The last thing she wanted to do was to look in the least vulnerable.

"You are looking well, Eden," Ben said, touching a hand to the soft, snow-white material that made up his headdress. He should have looked silly, or pretentious, dressed in his gray Armani suit, the headpiece held in place by two coils of something that looked very much like gold-wrapped silk, the edges of the material flowing over his shoulders.

But he didn't look silly. He looked wonderful. Dark, and mysterious, and somehow larger than life. Peter O'Toole as Lawrence of Arabia, but photographed in sepia tones. His eyes as dark as any Arabian night. His features chiseled from desert rock weathered by desert winds. His tall form muscular but not musclebound. His movements measured, graceful.

His hands...well, she already knew about his hands.

"And you. You're...um...you're looking well," she answered at last, then cleared her throat. Maybe the action would help her to breathe. But she doubted it. "You knew I'd be here today?"

"Yes, Eden, I did. A knowledge you obviously did not share."

Eden's temper hit her then, like a sharp slap on the back meant to dislodge a bit of stuck fish bone, or pride. "You're right, Your Highness. I had no knowledge that you'd be here today. That *Ben Ramsey* would be here today."

He bowed slightly, from the waist. A regal inclination, certainly no gesture that her words had impacted him, no sign of any reaction that had even a nodding acquaintance with the word "embarrassed."

She longed to clobber him with something hard and heavy.

And then he really blew her mind...

"Very well," he said coldly. "If you wish to play the ignorant, Eden, I suppose I am willing to listen as you tangle your tongue in knots, trying to deny that you did not know who I was—who I am. Or is your memory truly that faulty, that you forgot my letters, my explanations. That you forgot to answer those letters, just as you chose to forget me, forget Paris."

"Letters? What letters? The only letter I ever received from you was the note you left on the bed. Let's see, I think I still remember it. 'Eden, darling. I have been called home. Stay where you are, I shall contact you, explain everything as I should have at the beginning.' You signed it with love, as I recall."

She knew very well how he had signed the note, because she had kept it, for all of these years. It was all she could ever give Sawyer of his father.

The anger was back, cold and hard. "Did I know you were really a sheikh, Ben? How in hell was I supposed to know that? By reading between the lines of that note?"

When he said nothing, she stepped away from the table, picking up her attaché case as she headed past him toward the door. "I waited, Ben. I waited for nearly two weeks, long past the time I'd planned to return home, nearly too late to begin my next law school term. I waited, and I worried, and I finally realized that I knew nothing about you. Nothing important—like where you lived, if you had a family. If you had a wife. Finally, I woke up, realized I'd just had myself a Paris fling, and chalked you up to experience. And that's how I'd like to keep it, Ben. An experience in my past, one I'm in no mood to repeat."

He took hold of her elbow. Lightly, not really holding her in place, although she couldn't move. She was too shocked by the sensation his slight touch set off in her body, a warmth spreading throughout her, betraying her.

"I do not believe you have been asked to repeat it, Eden," he said quietly, his deep tones a seductive rumble low in his throat even as his words cut her, made her bleed. "But we are going to talk. Not here, not at this moment, but later. You will be at my hotel at six this evening, if you please. The Palace Lights here in San Antonio. Do you know it?"

"Oh, sure, like that's going to happen!" Eden shook herself loose from his grip, using much more force than was strictly necessary. "I wouldn't cross the street to see you, *Your Highness*. Put *that* in your…oh, hell, just stuff that in your *headpiece,* okay!''

She started for the door—when had the room grown so large?—but Ben spoke again, once more halting her in her tracks. ''You will please tell Attorney Klinger and the others that His Highness has decided not to open Kharmistan to foreign investors. You might call them foreign devils, or infidels, if you think it will help prove that this ignorant Arab has no business sense, no concept of the fortune he is turning down.''

Eden whirled back to face him, her blue eyes narrowed as her entire face pinched and blanched at the same time. ''You wouldn't dare,'' she said, her heart pounding so loud she could barely hear herself speak.

He turned to her slowly, his dark eyes cold, his face a mask of handsome, deeply tanned, unreadable flesh. ''If you have done your research, Eden, and I am convinced you have, you will know that I currently hold the position of twenty-third richest man in the world. I do not have much time for such lists, but they do seem to impress Westerners. So you see, Eden, I do not need your clients. I never did. I would not be here today if I had not seen your name on one of the status reports the faithful Nadim placed on my desk six months ago. He did not remember your name. I, however, have it branded on my heart.''

Eden refused to comment on his last statement. ''Six…six months ago? You've been planning all of this? Negotiating with our clients for six long months? Putting us all through hoops, acting as if you wanted this deal—all so you could come here today to insult me? Embarrass me? Why? Do you plan to have me lose my job? Is that it? Are you that petty? You've ignored me for more than five years. How does that end up being *my* fault?''

''Six o'clock, Eden.'' He walked past her and put his hand on the doorknob. ''Now, if you will excuse me? I have a meeting to postpone until tomorrow. It will only be postponed, will it not, Eden?''

Eden chewed on the inside of her cheek, longing to tell him to go to hell, longing to tell him she didn't give two snaps for the deal her firm had been working on for six long months. ''Yes, that's right. Only postponed, Your Highness,'' she ground out at last, then exited the room ahead of him as he held open the door and graciously gestured that she should precede him.

Mary Ellen Fortune poured two cups of tea in the large kitchen of the contemporary Colonial house she and her late husband had built on Fortune land several years earlier.

The house was only two miles from the original homestead that had been expanded to three or more times its size over the years. Not that Cameron had felt the huge, rambling house hadn't been large enough for he and Mary Ellen to raise their family there, alongside the family of his brother, Ryan.

Cameron had liked elegance, and size, and this house reflected his need for the overtly flamboyant and Mary Ellen's equal need to make a comfortable and cozy home within the parameters her husband had set up. Now, with the children grown and gone, with Cameron gone, the house she loved was too big, too empty.

"You and Sawyer could come here for a while, darling," Mary Ellen said as she carried the teacups to the wide butcher-block-topped kitchen table, placing one cup in front of Eden. "Security on the ranch is excellent, as you know. He couldn't touch Sawyer here."

Eden ran a hand through her hair, pushing the thick, wavy mass back from her face. She'd driven directly to the ranch as soon as the meeting had broken up, which it had done rapidly once Sheikh Barakah Karif Ramir had regally begged the kind indulgence of those gathered and then departed the room without so much as a word of excuse, surrounded by his phalanx of guards.

Eden had been so distracted that she couldn't

even remember what her boss had said to her, what he had asked her. She'd just sicced him on Jim Morris, and been the first person on the elevator when it returned to the twenty-sixth floor.

Her memory of locating her car in the underground parking lot, the drive to the Double Crown Ranch, to her mother's house, was equally vague. All she'd known was that she'd had to get to her mother, and she had to stay away from her own home on Edgewood Drive. Just in case she was followed...

"I can't stay here, Mom," Eden said, shaking her head. "Thanks to Ben—to the sheikh, that is—we're all meeting again tomorrow in San Antonio. I'd have to get up before dawn to make it into the city on time. But Sawyer could come here, couldn't he? He and Mrs. Betts."

"He could," Mary Ellen agreed, just as if she hadn't been the one to suggest the visit from her grandson. "And Mrs. Betts could watch him while I'm working. I have to get the quarterly reports in order soon, you know."

Eden nodded. Her mother had always been just that. A mother first and foremost, a loyal wife. But she also had a great business head that she'd employed to clean up after her husband's financial messes over the years.

With Cameron's death, she had stepped reluctantly into the limelight, and her business acumen had quickly landed her with new responsibilities and a reason to face life once more after her husband had gone.

"He wouldn't be a bother, Mom. He's got his pony up at the stables, but Mrs. Betts can drive him there whenever he wants…" Eden began, apologizing before the fact, but her mother waved off her weak words.

"I'm not saying I'm agreeing with you on this, Eden," Mary Ellen said, a hint of motherly sternness creeping into her voice. "But I know you've had a shock. The first thing you need to do is talk with this Ben Ramsey…this Sheikh Ramir. Straighten out what happened between you before Sawyer was born, learn more about these letters he swore he wrote to you, make your peace between you. Only then can you decide if you want to tell him of Sawyer's existence."

"You think I should, though, don't you?" Eden asked, grimacing as she looked at the clock on the wall, knowing she had to begin her drive back to San Antonio in the next fifteen minutes or she'd never be able to meet Ben at six o'clock, as he had ordered.

"He is the boy's father," Mary Ellen said, raising her teacup to her lips, then setting it down again. "I don't know that he deserves Sawyer, or that Sawyer deserves him, but I do know that Sawyer deserves some answers.''

Eden slumped against the back of the large wooden chair. "Oh, God.'' She lowered her head, rubbed at her forehead. "I'll send Mrs. Betts and Sawyer here directly after dinner tonight. That'll give me some time, and some distance. Unless he already knows…'' she said, her voice drifting off even as her head shot up and she looked at her mother.

"He could know, couldn't he? Once he'd seen my name he probably had someone make inquiries, check up on me, make sure I was the same Eden Fortune. Oh, God, Mom, why didn't I think of this before—he might already know!''

Two

Sheikh Barakah Karif Ramir entered the Palace Lights penthouse suite with the slow and measured step that reflected his life of patience, of waiting, of watching for the most opportune moment and then seizing that moment with both hands.

That was life in Kharmistan, the life of a prince, a sheikh. It was the life his late father had lived, and his father before him, for all of the sheikhs of Kharmistan who had known the feint and jab of politics, of intrigue, while these Americans were still learning how to build log cabins.

The sheikh had been raised at his father's knee, then sent off to be educated; first in England, later in America. He had not needed the education found in books, for there were books and teachers in Kharmistan. At the age of twelve he had been sent away to learn the ways of the world, of the men who were outside his father's small but strategically important kingdom.

Having an English mother had helped him, but nothing she had taught him could have prepared him for the lack of respect, mingled with hatred and misunderstanding, that had greeted him when he'd taken his first steps out of Kharmistan and into the world beyond his father's kingdom. In Kharmistan his family name was revered, honored, even feared. In England he was the outsider, the alien being, the oddity. His clothing was ridiculed, his speech pattern mocked.

That was when the young prince had learned the value of conformity, at least an outward conformity that seemed to put his classmates at ease.

He had forsaken his comfortable *tobe* and *kibr* for the short pants and blazer of his classmates, even though his father had gained permission for him to avoid the school uniform.

He had answered insults with a smile until he had found sticks big enough to beat them all down. Those sticks had been his brilliant horsemanship, his skill on the playing fields, his excellence in the classroom.

Within a year he had become the most popular student in the school, as well as its top student. He was invited to large country estates over term breaks, introduced to the sisters of his classmates, both welcomed and welcome wherever he went. His friends were legion, and they believed they knew him well.

They never knew him at all. But he knew them. He knew them very well.

What had begun so encouragingly in England had been equaled and then outdone by the success he had found in America during his years at Yale. He assimilated. He blended. He fit in. He became one of ''them,'' even though he was not one of them.

He could never be one of them, one of those he met, roomed with, ate with, laughed with over the years.

Because he was Barakah Karif Ramir, only son of the sheikh, heir to the throne of Kharmistan.

All his English and American friends knew him as Ben, the nickname his Yale roommate had given him when he could not remember how to pronounce Barakah.

And being Ben was easier, simpler. Nobody groveled, nobody harassed, nobody bothered to try to impress him or beleaguer him or ask anything of him.

It had been as Ben that he had traveled to Paris in an attempt, years after his return to Kharmistan, to recapture some of that simplicity that had been lost to him in the halls of his father's palace.

It had been as Ben that he had met Eden Fortune, the beautiful Texan he'd foolishly introduced himself to as Ben Ramsey. And why not? He'd anticipated an innocent flirtation, a Parisian romance, perhaps a mutually pleasurable dalliance.

Most women fawned all over him once they learned he was a prince. They fawned, and they preened, and they asked inane questions, and they got mercenary gleams in their beautiful eyes when they looked at him.

He had not wanted to see that acquisitional gleam in Eden Fortune's lovely blue eyes. And he had not. He had seen interest, yes. In time, he had seen love, a love he returned in full measure.

Even as he deceived her.

The summons back to Kharmistan had come too soon, before he could confess that deception, before he could ask her to marry him, share her life with him. A hurried note left on a pillowcase, and he was gone, flying back to Kharmistan on his private jet, racing to the bedside of his seriously ill father.

But he had written. He had written several times, little more than hurried notes scribbled between taking care of state business and sitting at his father's bedside. He had ordered those notes hand-delivered to Paris, with her replies placed directly into his hands.

Nothing.

There had been nothing.

No answer. No response.

And then she'd been gone. By the time he could

assure himself of his father's recovery and jet back to Paris, Eden had returned to America.

He may have let her believe he had never gotten a letter from her, but he had. The concierge at the hotel had handed him a small envelope when he had inquired about Eden at the front desk. *It's better this way. Eden.* He had taken that to mean that she'd wanted nothing to do with him once he had told her, in his letters, of his true identity, of the privilege and the burden that he carried as heir to the throne of Kharmistan.

For nearly six years he had believed he had done the right thing to walk away, to not look back. To forget. His father had never fully recovered from his stroke, and Ben had been forced to work night and day to try to fill his shoes, to keep their subjects calm, to eventually step into those shoes completely when his father died.

There had been no time for romance, for fond memories, for much of anything except the work of ruling his country.

He had married Nadim's daughter because it had been a politically advantageous move that had solidified the populace. But neither Leila nor Ben had been in love. Her death three years later had saddened him greatly, but he had barely noticed a difference in his always busy days. For he was the sheikh, and the sheikh lived for the state, not for personal happiness.

And then he had seen the memo from one Eden Fortune that Nadim had placed on his desk....

"Nadim?" he called out now as he went to the small bar in the corner of the living room of the suite, helping himself to an ice-cold bottle of spring water. "Nadim, are you there?"

A servant dressed in the traditional white linen *tobe,* his *kaffiyeh* secured to his head with an *agal* fashioned of thick woolen cords, appeared in the doorway, bowed to him. "His Excellency will be with you momentarily, Your Highness, and begs your pardon for inconveniencing you by even a moment's absence," he said, then bowed himself out of the room.

"Yeah, right," Ben muttered under his breath as he pulled the *kaffiyeh* from his own head, suddenly impatient with the formality with which he was treated as the Sheikh of Kharmistan. It was as if he lived inside a bubble, and no one was allowed to approach too closely, speak too plainly, say what the devil was on his or her mind.

He had a sudden longing for that long-ago summer in Paris, for the days and nights he had spent with Eden. That was probably because she had looked today as she had looked then, only even more beautiful, more assured, more amazingly intelligent and independent.

Although not so independent that she could refuse his request—his ultimatum—to come here tonight, to meet with him again. She had been angry with him, certainly, but she had also seemed frightened. Frightened for her job? No. It had been more than that, he was sure of it.

But what? What?

"Your Highness requested my presence? I ask forgiveness for being unprepared for your seemingly precipitate return. Things did not go so well at the meeting?"

Ben turned to look at his closest advisor. Yusuf Nadim was a tall, extraordinarily handsome man in his mid-sixties. Dark skin, dark hair without a strand of gray, a thin mustache over his full upper lip. Nadim wore Western clothing well, but seldom, and looked quite impressive now in his sheer white silk *kibr* ornamented with a gold neckband and tasseled cord. He wore the flowing *kibr* over a fine linen *tobe*. His *kaffiyeh* was constructed of the same sheer material as his *kibr,* and anchored in place with an elaborate *agal* wrapped in gold thread.

He bowed to Ben, but his dignity did not bow with him.

My third cousin, the man who would be sheikh, Ben thought idly, then dismissed the reflection as it did not give him pleasure. Neither did the subject at hand.

"You would like me to say yes, it did not go well. Would you not, Nadim?" Ben asked, smiling quite deliberately. "That way you could remind me of how very indispensable you are to the Sheikhs of Kharmistan, both to the father before him and now to the son. You could tell me how foolish I was to think I could negotiate a simple business deal without you by my side."

"On the contrary, Your Highness. I would never presume such a thing. I only ask, as advisor and father-in-law and friend, to humbly serve Your Highness with all of my feeble, unworthy self, in any way I can."

Nadim bowed again, but not before Ben saw the quick gleam of satisfaction—mingled with dislike?—in Nadim's dark eyes. He recalled his father's words on the subject of enemies. *It is best to keep them close, where you can watch them.*

Ben took another long drink of water, to cleanse his palate after Nadim's too sweet apology—or whatever the hell the man thought he had been offering. "I postponed the meeting until tomorrow, as something came up. Something unexpected," he told Nadim, effortlessly massaging the truth, "and unexpectedly personal."

"Your Highness?" Nadim asked, waiting to seat

himself until Ben had lowered himself onto one of the two striped couches in the living room area of the immense suite. The suite had six rooms, not counting those for the servants. Texans, it seemed, took great pleasure in living up to their reputation of "everything is bigger in Texas."

Ben pushed a hand through his coal-dark hair. Choosing his words carefully, he said, "Do you by chance remember an American woman by the name of Fortune, Nadim? Miss Eden Fortune?"

"A woman?" Clearly, Nadim was puzzled. "You postponed a meeting we have been planning for six months—for a woman? I know our beloved Leila is gone these past three years, Your Highness, but surely if you had need of a woman, there is no dearth of them at home in Kharmistan. If you had but asked, I—"

"There is a saying here in America, Nadim—'Get your mind out of the gutter.'" There was an edge of steel in Ben's voice as he interrupted the man. "You would do well to remember it."

Nadim inclined his head. "My profound apologies, Your Highness."

"Not that I am not honored by your offer to…um…*pimp* for your sheikh," Ben said, unable to hide his smile. "I had no idea that procuring willing females was part of your duties as my advisor."

Ben now saw the anger in Nadim's eyes, the fullness of it, the depth of it, even as the man answered with a smile of his own. "Your Highness is being droll."

"I try," Ben said, his own humor evaporating. "Now, to get back to Miss Eden Fortune, if I might. Do you recall the name?"

"I do not, Highness. I am sorry. Have I met the woman?"

Ben stood, walked over to stand in front of his advisor, looked down at him as he sat at his ease. "No, Nadim, you have not. Perhaps you remember my father's illness of some years ago, the time of his first cerebral accident?"

Nadim frowned as he stood, bowed to his sheikh. "Those were such trying times, Your Highness," he said apologetically. "Your father had been meeting with the various desert chieftains on the delicate matter of water rights when he collapsed, sending everyone into a panic. Fools, all of them, believing that Kharmistan could not survive your father's death. Our neighbors were looking for a reason to invade our territory, and without the loyalty of the chieftains we faced a turmoil that had to be avoided at all costs. We had to find you, which, I recall, was not an easy task, Your Highness, and then prominently produce you, prove that Kharmistan would go on, no matter what happened to your father."

"Then you do recall, Nadim," Ben said, beginning to pace once more. "And you found me. You found me in Paris. Now do you remember the name Eden Fortune?"

Nadim's eyes were as dark as a starless midnight in the Kharmistan desert. "The woman. Of course. The father on his sick bed, possibly his death bed, and the lovesick son passing notes like a schoolboy, demanding delivery by hand in Paris. How could I forget?"

Ben turned on his heels, looked straight at his father-in-law. "But you did as I said, didn't you, Nadim? You followed my direct order to have my letters hand-delivered to Miss Fortune in Paris?"

Nadim pulled his robe about him as he lifted his chin, struck a pose caught somewhere between arrogance and servility. "You question my loyalty, Your Highness? You question my vow to serve my prince in every way? I should leave your service at once, Your Highness, if you were to have lost confidence in me."

"I will consider that an answer in the affirmative, Nadim. You did send a messenger with my letters. They were, as you had promised me, delivered directly into her hands. I must believe that she lied to me this afternoon, for I cannot believe that my most trusted advisor lied to me six years ago, and is lying now even as he looks into the eyes of his sheikh."

Nadim continued to stare at Ben for long moments, then bowed, turned, and departed the room.

Ben's suspicions went with him.

Ben paced the living area of the penthouse suite, pretending he did not see the hands on the mantel clock, pretending he had not heard the clock strike six a quarter hour earlier.

She was not coming. He could not believe she would not come. Not because he had demanded her presence, but because of her loyalty to her employer. Even as he had fallen in love with Eden, he had been able to see her finer qualities with a calm and detached eye. Loyalty, he had been sure then, had been sure until fifteen minutes ago, was very important to Eden.

As he, obviously, was not. Had never been.

How strange, how odd, how unprepared Ben was for rejection. From the time he had been a child, he had only to crook his finger, raise his eyebrow, give the faintest hint of what—or who—he wanted, and all that he desired had simply dropped into his lap.

His birth counted for some of this, his personality and will to succeed accounted for more. From his excellence in sports to his conquests with women, he had only ever brushed up against failure, had never embraced it. Failure had never embraced him.

Except for Eden Fortune, in Paris.

Except for Eden Fortune, here in Texas.

And now what was he to do? If he backed out of the negotiations with the American triad, Eden would surely lose her position. Obviously he had not thought through his plan completely. After six long months of planning, he had failed to factor in Eden's temperament, her stubbornness in the face of his demands.

She was her own person. He had known that in Paris, he should have remembered it before he had presented her with an ultimatum that could only hurt any chance he had of speaking with her, perhaps holding her again. Perhaps loving her again.

"Stupid!" Ben told himself as he reached up a hand to his sheer *kaffiyeh* with its bold black *agal*. He had been as stupid, as cowhanded, with Eden as he had been to have dressed himself in the brilliantly striped *aba* denoting him as sheikh, a move meant to impress her, perhaps intimidate her.

Before he could yank the *kaffiyeh* from his head, strip off the *aba* to reveal the more pedestrian slacks and knit shirt beneath it, the doorbell of the suite buzzed once, twice.

"Eden," Ben breathed, relaxing his shoulders, realizing that he, who routinely stared down princes, had been both anticipating and dreading this meeting. He was on edge, nervous. And that made him angry.

He walked over to stand in front of the floor-to-ceiling windows looking out over the city as one of the servants opened the door to the tiled foyer and he heard Eden give the man her name.

"Miss Eden Fortune, Highness," the servant said a moment later, bowing Eden into the room, then retiring as he earlier had been bidden. Haskim would be back in a half hour, to serve the dinner of Middle Eastern specialities Ben had ordered prepared in the suite kitchen. Ben had, with an inner smile, ordered *Dolma*—stuffed grape leaves—among other Middle Eastern specialties, just to see how Eden reacted when she took her first bite of the delicacy that was a bit of an acquired taste.

Now he felt petty, and wished he had ordered from the hotel kitchens. Not that Nadim would allow such a thing without making a great fuss out of being his official taster, just in case the hotel chef had tried to poison the Sheikh of Kharmistan. The last person Ben wanted present in the room tonight was his outwardly conscientious, inwardly jealous father-in-law.

Ben watched as Eden walked into the room, her head held high, her posture that of a soldier about to undergo inspection. She was still clothed in the same trim, prim navy-blue suit he had seen her in this morning. Ben considered the outfit to be a deliberate choice, one meant to show her disdain for him, her determination to make this a business meeting and nothing more.

"Your Highness," she said with a barely perceptible inclination of her head as she stopped, folded her hands in front of her. Glared at him.

Her dark brown hair was still drawn back severely. A French twist, Ben believed the style was called. He wondered if Eden could appreciate the irony in that description. The severe hairstyle helped to accentuate Eden's high cheekbones, the clean sweep of her jaw, the fullness of her lips. Just as the severe blue suit skimmed over her body, setting off memories, hinting of a promise Ben was sure Eden had no intention of declaring.

She was magnificent. From her pride to her delicious body, she was magnificent. Just as he remembered her. Just as he had never been able to forget her.

Her blue eyes sparkling with anger and a hint of fear he could not like, she gestured to the couches, saying, "If the inspection is over, would it be possible for the two of us to sit down, discuss our problems like adults?"

"I have no intention of reneging on the deal with the clients your law firm represents, Eden," he said immediately, hoping to see some of the starch leave her slim shoulders. "I can only ask your forgiveness for such a heavy-handed threat, but in my stupidity

I could not think of another way to convince you to have dinner with me tonight.''

Eden sat, sliding her hands along her thighs as she did so, smoothing down her skirt. ''You could have asked me, Ben,'' she said bluntly. ''That's how we do it here. You ask, I answer.''

''In the affirmative?''

Her chin lifted a fraction. ''Hardly. I much prefer to keep our association limited to business.''

Ben sat on the facing couch, smiled. ''Then I withdraw my apology, for I was determined that we should meet privately. I regret that you only agreed under duress, but I am equally determined to enjoy the evening.''

As if on cue, one of the kitchen servants—Nadim insisted they travel with a full staff—bowed himself into the room, carrying a heavy silver tray laden with a sampling of Middle Eastern appetizers, including the *Dolma*.

''It all looks delicious, thank you,'' Eden told the servant, who bowed to her then asked Ben if he could be permitted to serve them with cold juices freshly squeezed in the kitchen. Ben agreed, and the servant bowed again, backing out of the room.

''I thought he was going to kiss your feet,'' Eden said, sitting forward on the couch and picking up a small china plate as her free hand hovered over the assortment of appetizers. ''Oh, *Dolma*. I adore stuffed grape leaves, don't you? And what's that?'' she asked, pointing to another dish. "I don't think I recognize that one.''

"A sampling of *Maldhoom*," Ben said, watching as Eden popped a grape leaf into her mouth, closed her eyes as she savored the taste. "It is made of eggplant and a variety of seasonings. I can ask my cook to write down the recipe if you like.''

Eden wrinkled her nose. Just the way she'd wrinkled her nose at that small restaurant on the West Bank of Paris as she watched him eat his way through a plateful of snails. "Eggplant? Thanks, but I'll pass. But these are eggrolls of some kind, aren't they?''

"*Shamboorek,*" Ben told her, wondering how he could have forgotten how dedicated Eden could be to good food. "We have many varieties of eggrolls, but these, I do believe, are stuffed with ground lamb, onion, and seasoned with a variety of spices.''

Eden nodded her understanding, wiping her fingers on one of the linen napkins placed on the tray, then dabbing the napkin at her chin, which had collected a bit of the sauce from the *Dolma*. She took a sip of apple juice the servant had placed in front of her, then reached for the *Shamboorek*.

She had the eggroll halfway to her mouth before she stopped, looked at him, and a very becoming blush colored her cheeks. "I'm so sorry. I haven't eaten more than a few bites all day for one reason or another. I can't believe I'm diving in like this!"

"But understandable. The fuller the mouth, the less one can be made to speak," Ben said, lifting a glass of chilled apple juice to his own lips.

"What's that, Ben?" Eden asked, putting the egg-roll back on the plate. "Some kind of ancient proverb? If it is, I don't like it."

"Again, my apologies. And, please, continue to enjoy the food. I can remember now how much joy food gives you. A woman who enjoys the pleasures of the senses, and is not ashamed to indulge herself. Do you remember the night I fed you fresh strawberries in cream, Eden? How you licked the cream from my fingers, how I kissed the tart juice on your lips? So innocently sensual, so impossible to forget."

"That's it!" Eden said, tossing down her napkin. She stood, with only one quick, longing look toward the plate of *Shamboorek*. "I came, we spoke, and now I'm leaving. I'll see you in the morning, Your Highness. And then I'll count myself lucky if I never have to see you again!"

"Your Highness?"

Ben turned to see three of his servants standing in the hallway, one of them with sword already drawn. "We heard the raising of voices, Your Highness," Haskim said. "There is trouble?"

Ben grinned up at Eden, who was glaring at the servants with enough anger in her eyes to most probably stop a charging rhino in its tracks. "Do you want to see what would happen if I were to say 'Sic her, boys'?" he murmured quietly, so that only Eden could hear. "Or maybe you would just rather sit down once more, and enjoy your *Shamboorek.*"

As Eden stood, and steamed, Ben waved the servants out of the room, wondering just how far Nadim had told them to go, how close Nadim had ordered them to stay.

With that thought in his mind, he excused himself from Eden and followed after the servants, shooing them along in front of him until they stood in front of the door to the kitchen. "You insult me, believing your sheikh could be overpowered by one small female," he said sternly, then smiled. "Go eat your dinner, all right?"

He stopped to discard the *kaffiyeh* and *aba* on a chair in the hallway, smoothed his hair, and reentered the living room of the suite, saying, "I have convinced my attendants that you are not hiding a Glock under your jacket or a bomb in your purse. Although I would suggest you not raise your voice again, not if you want my servants to partake of their evening meal in peace."

"You're enjoying this, aren't you?" Eden snapped, picking up an eggroll and taking a whopping great bite out of it. She spoke around a mouthful of pastry and meat. "I see you lost the robe and...and headdress. When are you going to bring out the crown jewels, or the scepter, or whatever else in hell you think would impress me with how terrific you are?"

"I was trying to impress you, I admit it," Ben said honestly. "But, as I could see it did not work, I decided to make myself more comfortable."

"Well, bully for you. *I'm* not comfortable! Ben Ramsey, garden variety lawyer on vacation. Ha! I can't believe I fell for that—although no one could blame me for not knowing you were really Sheikh Barakah Karif Ramir, now could they? I mean, how many sheikhs can ten thousand vacationing college girls hope to meet? What are the odds? But now, since we seem to be firmly on the subject I really didn't want to talk about, let me take a wild guess as to why you left. You have a wife, don't you, Ben? Or maybe six of them?"

"I have been married since last I saw you, Eden, and widowed three years ago. We had no children. But do not believe all you hear about sheikhs and harems, if you please. It makes for titillating press, but is far from the truth."

"Widowed?" Eden bowed her head for a moment, then looked at him levelly. "I'm sorry, Ben, I didn't know. It's a good thing I don't have any more eggroll in my mouth. It leaves more room for my foot.''

''An apology, Eden? I accept it with pleasure.'' He sat once more, deftly picked up a grape leaf and popped it into his mouth. ''So, are we being sociable now?''

''Sociable, Ben? I don't know about that. But I suppose we could be civil, at the very least.'' She sat back against the couch cushions, smiled at him. ''So, how have you been? Is it difficult? Being a sheikh, that is. I should imagine it could be rather suffocating, if this evening's events are any indication.''

''I manage,'' he told her, ''although I have never again been able to sneak away to Paris, as I did before my father died.''

''Died? Was that why you deserted…uh…why you left Paris so abruptly? Your father died?''

''He became quite ill, and never fully recovered until his death some six months later. That much is true. But I did not desert you, Eden. I wrote, had letters hand-delivered to your hotel. Those letters you told me today you had never received.''

''And I didn't!'' Eden declared, then winced, lowered her voice. ''Sorry. I wouldn't want to see the cavalry showing up again.''

''I wrote three letters, Eden,'' he continued as she wiped at her fingers, avoided his eyes. ''Three. Each one explaining who I was, why I had to leave. Three letters personally placed in my chief advisor's hand and then couriered to Paris by one of his staff. And I saw your answer when I could at last return to Paris myself. How did it go? Oh, yes. Some nonsense about it being 'better' this way. Was it better that way, Eden? Better that you should leave, turn your back on what we had?''

Eden continued to stare at him, her blue eyes as honest as they were beautiful. ''I never saw any letters from you, Ben. I already told you that. And you believe me, don't you? You might not have believed me this morning, but you believe me now. What did you do, Ben, turn your trusted advisor over to the thumbscrews?''

''I am considering having him smeared with honey, staked out on the desert, and nibbled to death by toothless camels, even though I am sure he believes he was acting in the best interests of Kharmistan,'' Ben said fatalistically, accepting what was impossible to change, as his father had taught him. Then he smiled, sadly. ''All these years, Eden. Lost to both of us.''

Eden sighed, shook her head. ''Not to you, Ben. You became a sheikh, a great prince. You married. I doubt you gave me a thought until you saw my name as you looked over the oil and gas deal. Just as I put my memories of you in my past and got on with my life.''

''Dinner is now to be served, if it is your pleasure, Your Highness,'' Haskim said as he entered the room.

Ben continued to stare at Eden for another long moment, watching a flush kiss her cheeks as she so obviously lied to him. ''Thank you, Haskim. Will you please be so kind as to seat Miss Fortune in the dining room? I will join her shortly.''

''Ben—I mean, Your Highness?'' Eden said, her voice clouded by concern. ''You—you aren't going to fire the man or anything like that? Anything *worse* than that? I mean, you have absolute power, don't you? I'm sure I read that somewhere in my notes.''

Ben stood as Eden did, motioned for her to follow Haskim into the dining room. ''You overreact, Eden. I have a call coming from Kharmistan precisely at seven, and it is nearing that hour now. When I have completed my conversation with my minister of water and power, I shall join you. All right?''

''But I can see how angry you are, Ben. Like that day I was nearly run down by a horse-drawn carriage as we walked through Paris. Your eyes are all dark, the way they were then, and I can see a vein pulsing at the side of your throat. Please, don't do anything rash. What's done is done, and I'm sure your advisor had very good reasons for disobeying you. You said that, didn't you? That he must have had the best interests of Kharmistan in mind?''

"You are much more forgiving than I am, Eden," Ben said, pushing his temper back under his usual tight control, trying once more to remember his father's words. He had suspected so earlier, but it was only Eden's honesty tonight that finally convinced him that Nadim had disobeyed his direct orders. "There will be a punishment, I assure you, but I will listen first, then act. And I must act, Eden, as any show of weakness in one's sheikh is reason to believe in one's own ambitions. Nadim would expect no less from me. Is that all right with you?''

Eden licked at her lips, eyed him nervously. "I— I suppose so, Ben. And you'll join me shortly? After your phone call?''

Another servant entered the room, carrying a portable phone on a lace doily placed in the center of a silver tray. Ben picked up the phone, nodded to Eden, then turned his back to her, speaking a fast and fluent Arabic into the phone.

Three

My son cannot live in Ben's world. Eden's head hurt as the message repeated itself in her brain. Her stomach had turned to stone, her appetite gone. All she could do was sit in the dining room chair, her hands folded tightly in her lap, while her mind began to scream, *Run away, run away, run away.*

She could run to the ends of the earth. But this time, Ben would come after her. Ben would find her. If he knew about Sawyer, he would find her.

She might have told Ben Ramsey about his son, about Sawyer. She could have seen herself doing just that, had imagined the scenario many times over the years.

"We may not have done anything else right, Ben," she would have said to him, "but, between us, we created one terrific kid. You have a right to know that."

She could have said that to Ben Ramsey, if he'd shown up on her doorstep one day, if she'd known where to look to find him.

But she could not tell Sheikh Barakah Karif Ramir that he had a young prince residing in San Antonio, going to preschool three mornings a week; that his favorite pastime was watching a television show featuring talking locomotive engines, that he slept with his thumb in his mouth and a bear named Fred clutched in his arms.

She could not tell this prince, this sheikh, this omnipotent king, that he had sired a sweet, wonderful, normal little boy who spoke with a slow Texas drawl.

Eden kept her eyes downcast, very much aware that the servant, Haskim, remained in the dining room, watching her as if she might be contemplating secretly pocketing the solid silver utensils on either side of her plate.

And she continued to think, continued to panic.

What would Sawyer look like in one of those headdresses, one of those colorful robes?

God. He'd look just like his father, that's what he'd look like. A miniature of his father, complete with princely bearing.

She'd lose Sawyer. If Ben found out about their son, he would demand the child be taken to Kharmistan, educated in Kharmistan, prepared for the day he would replace his father as sheikh.

Her little boy. Her sweet, wonderful, innocent little baby. A pawn in a political game played in a very political country. A hostage to fortune, cementing Ben's rule, securing the succession.

She couldn't tell Ben. She had to hide Sawyer, hide him until Ben left the country. There was no other way.

And she had to hide herself, as well. She couldn't let him too close, couldn't let him see how much his reentry into her life had shaken her, had started her dreaming foolish, romantic dreams she'd thought long ago left behind her in Paris.

Her head came up with a jerk as Haskim bowed from the waist, signaling that Ben had entered the room. Eden blinked back frightened tears and looked at him, looked at Sawyer's father.

She had tried to forget him. She had tried to forget how much she had loved him.

She might love him still, she most probably would always love him…but now she feared him more.

"Was your phone call successful?" she asked as Haskim held out a chair and Ben sat across from her. "Or perhaps I shouldn't ask?"

"You can ask me anything you want, Eden," Ben told her as a flurry of servants and serving trays almost magically produced a table heavily laden with a half-dozen different plates holding different Middle Eastern delicacies. "I may not, however," he added, smiling, "always give you answers. Now, shall we eat?"

Eden, believing she would most probably choke on water, spread her hands, indicating the diverse dishes in front of her. "Everything smells delicious, Ben, but I would like you to explain the dishes, if you would?"

"Certainly, although your familiarity with Dolma had me mistakenly believing that you already had a knowledge of my country's food. This," he said, indicating the large platter just in front of him, "is *Beriani*, a traditional chicken dish made with cloves, cinnamon, rice, potatoes, and a few hard-boiled eggs. There's more to it than that, of course, including many other spices. You may want to give it a small taste before committing yourself to it, unless you enjoy what I believe you call 'hot' dishes?"

The change of subject gave Eden what she needed, something to hang her mind on so that she would not worry that she'd open her mouth at any moment and blurt out Sawyer's name. "You're speaking to a Texan, born and bred, Ben, remember? I'll pit our salsa against your *Beriani*, and see who's the first to reach for the ice water. Now, what else is here?"

In quick order Ben recited the names of the other dishes. The red lentil soup Haskim placed in front of them both, called *Adas* soup. A second chicken entrée, this one prepared with ginger and garbanzo beans. Stuffed eggplant, which he called *Sheikh*

Mehshee. Eden wrinkled her nose at that one, asking that he not put any of it on her plate, thank you.

There was *Kibbi,* a mixture of bulgur, wheat and lamb. Some was served with the meat raw, some had been formed into patties and cooked to a dark brown. Lastly, an easily recognized leg of lamb, called *Koozy,* also served with rice cooked in Middle Eastern spices, and sprinkled with plump, cooked raisins.

"There's enough food here to feed half of the city," Eden told him at last, shaking her head.

"Yes, I know," Ben replied, placing a healthy slice of lamb on her plate. "And I cannot begin to tell you how I long for a fast-food hamburger, some extremely greasy French fries, and perhaps a home-delivered pizza with pepperoni and mushrooms."

Eden chewed on a piece of meat, amazed at how good it tasted, delighted that she could swallow it. "You're the sheikh, Ben, for crying out loud. Can't you get the limo to stop at The Golden Arches? The limo would be a real hoot at the drive-thru. Or maybe you could order one of your servants to dial the local pizza shop?"

"Eden," he said rather indulgently, "have you really looked around you? Really seen how I am catered to, fussed over, worried about? Haskim and his staff scoured the city all day yesterday, looking for the correct ingredients for tonight's dinner, hoping to prove to me their loyalty, their ingenuity, their worthiness to serve their sheikh. I cannot disappoint them by announcing that I wish for a hot dog. I can, however, ask you if you would be willing to play hooky after tomorrow morning's meeting, so that you can show me your city…and your restaurants.''

''I—I don't know…I mean, there's the meeting…and then all the work back at the office after the meeting, and…well, I don't think I can. And you'll be leaving for Kharmistan very soon after that, won't you?''

Eden closed her eyes, knowing she had just shown herself to be terrified of being in Ben's company. Why hadn't she offered to drive him to his plane, help him board, wave him off? She couldn't have been less subtle.

''Actually, Eden, I will be staying in Texas for some time, perhaps as long as a few weeks,'' Ben told her as her smile froze to her face. ''I am interested in purchasing a few horses of diverse background and training for my private stable. And, of course, I am looking forward to spending more time with you, if you will agree. So you see, I have combined this business visit with my own pleasure.''

''Oh. That's nice,'' Eden said weakly, poking her fork into a single plump raisin, then raising it to her mouth. ''And yet, sometimes it's safe—er, better to be content with memories, don't you think? And, besides, I'm beginning a week's vacation on Friday afternoon, and will be visiting my mother, so it will be rather impossible, although I thank you for thinking of me.''

"You are afraid of me.''

Eden realized she hadn't looked directly at Ben since he had served her food. She raised her head, looked at him as levelly as she could muster, and said, ''Of course not! I'm not at all afraid of you. What gave you that idea?''

"If not me, Eden, then perhaps you are afraid of you. Is that it? Are the memories crashing in, as they are overtaking me? The need to remember, to hold on to the dream, to test it here in reality?''

Her control snapped. "You abandoned me!''

"You know that is not true.''

"You didn't come to America to look for me.''

"I believed your wishes were that I should not pursue you.''

"But you knew where I was.''

"Yes. Harvard. I knew that much. I could have found you.''

"But you were too gentlemanly to come after me? Too disinterested to come to me, to talk to me, to make me listen to you, understand?''

"My father was dying, Eden. I believed you had received my letters, my explanations, and determined that my true identity, and my responsibilities, were too much for you. My heart was divided, as I felt I could persuade you differently, but my mind knew where I was needed most.''

Eden exhaled shakily, dropping her elbow to the tabletop and resting her forehead in her hand. ''This is too much. Too much to assimilate, to even begin to understand. You never meant to leave me. You would have followed if I had given a single hint that I wished to be pursued. You married, were widowed. And now you're acting as if we can just pick up where we left off in Paris—as if we've not been living separate lives for more than five years. Dammit, Ben, I feel like I've been beaten with sledgehammers ever since I first saw you this morning.''

Ben spoke again, and she flinched, realizing that he had left his chair, was now standing beside her. ''We loved once, Eden, and we lost. Through misunderstanding, through misguided loyalty on the part of my advisor, through my own pride, which is considerable. There is an empty place inside of me, Eden, one that has not been filled since last I saw you, since last I held you, loved you.''

She twisted her head so that her cheek pressed against her palm, and looked up at him, grimaced. ''Oh, you're good. I'll give you that, Ben. You don't need the headdress or the robe or the servants or the food. You're really very good, all by yourself.''

''I am also determined, Eden, and I believe you

know that, as well,'' he told her, stroking his hand down her cheek, trailing his fingers across her exposed throat. "Now, I shall return to my seat and we will attempt to please my servants by the strength of our appetites. Although you must remember to save some of that appetite for the desserts soon to come. We will have *Klaichah,* delicious cookies stuffed with dates, and sesame cookies, which we call *Semsemia.* And, of course, *Baklava.* You do know *Baklava,* don't you, Eden?''

"I know *Baklava,* Ben,'' Eden told him dully, feeling herself drowning in a veritable sea of foreign-sounding names, foreign-tasting foods. "And that's about all I do know right now.''

"That is all either of us has to know, Eden, for now. Tomorrow will arrive soon enough, and with it another chance for us, a chance to begin again. We both deserve that chance, do we not?''

She looked at him, really looked at him. He'd aged a little in the past years, with a few more wrinkles around the outside corners of his eyes, a few new lines bracketing his wide, full lips. There was even the small beginnings of silver at his temples. But he was still Ben. Not her Ben, not the Ben Ramsey she'd known and loved in Paris. But he was still the same man, and held the same attraction she had felt so immediately when they'd met.

"We'll talk more tomorrow, all right? That's all

I can promise,'' she said at last, wincing as Haskim placed a small tower of honey-topped, diamond-shaped *Baklava* on the table.

Ben was right. She'd kill for a cheeseburger.

And safety.

Eden knew she wasn't about to get either....

''You!''

Ben had been standing in front of the large windows overlooking the city. Waiting. Biding his time. He turned now, at the sound of Eden's voice, bowing as he acknowledged her entrance into the small antechamber adjoining the main meeting room.

He had withdrawn here purposely, giving her time with her colleagues after their early morning meeting, time to collect the signed contracts, time to relax a little, to swallow, and at least partially digest her success before she was given the news that was sure to anger her.

After all, if she had to chase him down, follow him back to his hotel, she might implode before she could explode.

''Eden,'' he said smoothly, surprised no smoke was coming out of her ears, wondering how far the fuse of her temper had burned down, how long he would have to wait for the first glimpse of flame. ''I believed I had signed everything in all the correct places. Is there something else?''

She raised a hand, wagged a finger at him a time or two, then snapped her mouth shut, shook her head. "Never mind, I'm outta here," she declared, turning to leave the room once more.

"You spoke with your employer, Attorney Klinger?" Ben goaded, his pride still slightly chafed by her refusal to give him a definitive answer to the questions he had asked her the previous evening.

Sheikh Barakah Karif Ramir was not accustomed to begging. He was accustomed to giving orders, and Attorney Klinger, it seemed, was accustomed to granting favors for those who helped him collect immense fees from his grateful clients.

"Did I speak to Attorney Klinger," Eden parroted, turning back and slamming her attaché case down on the table as she glared at Ben. "You know damn well I spoke with him. Just like you know damn well that you spoke with him. Threatened him, I'll bet."

"I never threaten, Eden," he answered her smoothly. "I have never found threats necessary."

"No, you wouldn't, would you?" She was all but sneering now, and he longed to pull her into his arms, calm her with kisses. "You don't have to threaten. People just fall over themselves offering you anything you want. Well, don't look now, Ben, but you just met the exception!"

"You always were, Eden," Ben told her, walking

across the room to pick up her attaché case, hand it to her. "Now, as Attorney Klinger was generous enough to reward you with four extra days of holiday, beginning at this moment, and as his only request to you was that you show me a bit of your lovely city before I return to Kharmistan, perhaps you would be so kind as to join me for a Texas lunch. I have heard very interesting things about something called a fajita. I understand it partially consists of a form of unleavened bread, such as our own pita bread."

"That's not going to happen. So why don't you just take your sneaky maneuvers, Ben, and stick them in your *kaffiyeh*," Eden all but growled.

"A *kaffiyeh*, Eden? You took the time to learn the proper name for my headdress between last night and this morning? I am flattered."

"Don't be. Anyone can look up information on the Internet, and the information was for my own benefit, not yours. And now I am leaving—alone," she said, grabbing her attaché case out of his hand and all but running from the room.

Ben followed more slowly, taking his time with a flurry of formal bows and stilted farewells the Texans seemed to believe necessary.

Surrounded by his phalanx of bodyguards, he entered the elevator when it returned to the twenty-sixth floor, then stepped out into the lobby, his pace still measured as he walked outside to his limousine.

Eden was standing there, waiting for him, just as he had known she would be.

No, he never threatened. But he had frightened Eden, how he was not quite sure, and she would only run so far before she stopped to see if he was pursuing her.

If he only knew why.

"You reached for the ice water first, remember," Eden teased as she and Ben walked out of the small family-run Tex-Mex restaurant. "Which means you owe me a dollar."

"I do?" Ben questioned her, shaking his head, now devoid of his *kaffiyeh,* which he had left behind in the limousine. "I do not remember a wager, Eden."

"I'm a Fortune, Ben, and we're all born gamblers, in one way or another. So there's always a reward for winning. In this case, I've decided a dollar will do it."

Ben reached into his pockets and came out empty. "May I owe it to you, Eden? I am afraid I must admit that I never carry money with me."

"Yes, I noticed that inside when Haskim stepped forward to pay the bill. How do you stand it? I'd feel naked without my purse, my wallet."

Ben shook his head at the limousine driver and took Eden's arm, guiding her down the sunlit sidewalk in the direction of the famed San Antonio Riverwalk. "I have never thought about it, actually. I do not think I have handled a single coin since becoming sheikh. Money has always simply appeared when I needed it."

"Money appears, Ben, because you're smart and savvy and you just worked an extraordinary oil and gas deal that benefits our side, definitely, but which positively heaps money into your pockets—or wherever you keep it."

She looked down nervously, to where his hand cupped her elbow, and then at the street in front of him. "Where are we going?"

"Touristing," he answered easily, approaching a small, flat boat beside a sign offering tours of the area. He held up a hand and Haskim stepped forward, already reaching into his pocket. "I will take that, Haskim," he said, relieving the servant of the fat wallet and then dismissing him for the remainder of the afternoon. He had already dismissed the rest of his guards, who had been unhappy to obey him but seemed to find it impossible to not obey him.

"But, Your Highness," Haskim bleated between bows. "His Excellency will ask where it is you are, and I will have to say that I do not know, that I was dismissed."

"Ben?" Eden prodded, giving him a slight jab in his side with her elbow. "Do something. You're going to get Haskim in trouble."

Ben looked up and down the Riverwalk, smiling as he came to a conclusion. "You have a watch, Eden?" When she lifted her wrist to show him that she did, he unstrapped his gold Rolex watch and handed it to Haskim, along with half a dozen hundred-dollar bills. "It is now two, Haskim. Meet us here, at this exact spot, at five, with your arms full of presents you will be taking home to Bashiyra and your children."

"Your Highness is too kind," Haskim said, once more bowing to his sheikh. "But His Excellency—"

"His Excellency knows only what we tell him, Haskim. Surely you do not feed him the events of my day each evening along with his sweet tea?"

Haskim shifted his eyes from side to side, his features darkening as Eden took a step forward, looking at him closely. "I serve my sheikh, Your Highness. I serve you."

"How comforting. Now, run along. We will see you at five."

Ben watched Eden watch the servant leave. Her blue eyes were shadowed, her expression one of concern. Concern mixed with what he was sure could only be fear. Concern he would have appreciated. He did not appreciate the fear. "Is there something wrong?"

She looked up at him, wet her lips. "You don't see it? I watched your associate this morning, Ben, the man Haskim refers to as 'His Excellency.' Yusuf Nadim, your chief assistant or advisor or whatever you want to call him. And, as you said, I did do some more homework last night, learning more on the internet than the word *kaffiyeh*."

"And you are about to share this new knowledge with me?"

"You already know it," Eden said as Ben peeled bills from the thick wad and presented them to the man at the small boat dock.

"We will rent the entire boat," he said, his tone—and the bills—not allowing for argument. He then helped Eden into the boat, motioned for her to sit before joining her on one of the long benches.

"This is decadent," Eden said, looking around, and flushing with embarrassment as the boat pushed away from the dock with its two passengers when it could have easily held thirty tourists. "But let's not change the subject, all right?"

Ben took her hand, lifted it to his lips. "I would not dream of doing any such thing, Eden. Especially as you are about to tell me something you say I already know."

"Ha, ha," Eden said grimly, her body relaxing a

little as she leaned over the side of the flat-bottomed boat to trail her fingertips in the water as they passed by quaint hotels that lined the Riverwalk. "What I know—what you know, is that Yusuf Nadim is—was—your father-in-law. That he has been chief advisor to your father, and now serves you in the same capacity. And that he is not without ambition."

"Poor, hopefully devious, painfully obvious Nadim. He positively oozes ambition from every pore," Ben agreed genially. "You did not like him?"

"I don't trust him, Ben. There's a big difference. I don't know him well enough to not like him. Has there ever been a coup in Kharmistan?"

"A successful one? Not since my great-great-grandfather took over the throne, no. Do you think I should be watching my back, Eden? Is that what you are saying?"

She lifted her hand out of the water, looked up at the scenery passing by. "I don't know what I'm saying, Ben. I just get the feeling that you don't trust your own closest advisor. I also get the feeling that, while you don't trust him, you also don't fear him. Is that wise?"

Ben blew his breath out slowly, shaking his head. "Americans. Always looking for intrigue. Do you really see us all as bloodthirsty savages creeping through our desert palaces, armed to the teeth and out to slice off somebody's head?''

"Don't insult me or your own people, Ben," Eden said, stiffening as she sat close beside him. ''I'm not saying that Nadim is about to murder you in your bed. What I am saying is that I don't think he'd be devastated if you were to somehow lose your subjects' esteem and they went looking around for a new sheikh.''

"Lose the esteem of my subjects?'' Ben thought about this for a moment, then smiled. "You mean, by taking an American wife?''

If they had not been on a boat, gliding down the center of the slim river, Ben was sure Eden would have leaped to her feet, preparing to make another of her dramatic exits. As it was, she left him to sit on the facing bench, her wonderful blue eyes shooting sparks that should have set his hair ablaze.

"I don't want to talk about this anymore, Ben. I thought we had called a truce of some sort—even if I had to come to the peace table under the threat of you telling my boss that I wasn't being a good, co-operative little corporate lawyer. I was enjoying your company. But marriage? That's ridiculous, and you know it. I never thought about that for a moment.''

"That is unfortunate, but I hope not impossible to contemplate sometime in the future. In the meantime, may I tell you that my late mother was British? She and my father were married for nearly thirty years before she died, without causing a single insurrection. If that eases your mind at all.''

''It would ease my mind to be off this boat and in a cab heading away from you,'' she shot back, her cheeks still flushed, although more with embarrassment than anger. At least he hoped this was so.

They moved through the water, watching the passing scenery without speaking, until Ben finally stood, joined her on the long bench.

In a voice meant not to be overheard, he said, ''I had a long conversation with Nadim last evening, Eden. A long, rather probing conversation in which he finally admitted that he had not had my messages delivered to you in Paris. His reasoning was sound, if I remembered the unease in my country at the time, the worry over my father's health, the succession, the chance of invasion by bordering countries if we showed even a hint of vulnerability.''

''He wasn't up to having to deal with a lovesick prince mooning after an American? He worried that you might return to Paris, show yourself to be a playboy prince, or perhaps a man who was no longer in touch with the wishes and hopes of his father's subjects?''

Ben shook his head, smiling. ''I might have couched all of that in terms more flattering to me, I believe. But you are correct. If I had left Kharmistan again, followed after you to America, and my father had died—well, it was much easier to remove the threat than to deal with the consequences. At least, to Nadim's mind it was.''

"He was perfectly polite to me this morning," Eden said slowly, as if still considering Nadim's behavior and finding that politeness on the advisor's part did not equal trust on hers.

"I am secure, Eden, my throne is secure. We are a small but peaceful country. When the time comes, and I have a son, his future will be secure. Nadim's hopes for the throne died with my wife Leila, who had not yet produced the grandson Nadim would tutor, would coach, would do his best to control. He is a bitter man.''

"That's cold," Eden said, abruptly pulling back her hand as Ben tried to take it in his. "That he would marry his daughter to you for his own ambition. And that you would let him."

Now Ben did take hold of both her hands, holding them tightly as he looked deep into her eyes. "You were gone, Eden. You wanted nothing to do with a prince, an heir to a sheikhdom. This is what I thought as I agreed to the marriage with Leila, a purely political union we both understood when we agreed to the marriage."

"I can't understand that sort of thinking, Ben,"

Eden said, her voice small and filled with feeling. "I can't get my mind around your culture, the duties of a sheikh, the personal sacrifices that must be made in the name of preserving what sounds to me like a golden prison. I mean, money and titles didn't do a whole heck of a lot for Princess Di, now did they?"

"I understand what you are saying, Eden," Ben said as the boat pulled back to the dockside and they prepared to climb onto the cobbled Riverwalk. "I also understand that I am moving too swiftly, without a single thought to anything but the need to erase the mistakes and lost years, to begin again, if we can."

Her hands were on his shoulders as he lifted her out of the boat by cupping his hands around her waist. He pulled her close, looked down at her, felt the need to hold her, to kiss her.

And fought that need, knowing that he had come far enough in the past twenty-four hours, knowing that he had probably traveled too far, too fast.

Eden matched him look for look, her blue eyes shining with unshed tears, her hands trembling as they gripped his shoulders.

He needed. He wanted.

And he was frightening her because they both knew she also needed. Also wanted.

"Shall we visit some of the shops, Eden?" he

asked lightly, taking her hand in his as they began walking toward the line of small stores they had passed earlier on their way from the restaurant. "I have begun nurturing a nearly overwhelming desire to present my entire staff with cowboy hats. Very large cowboy hats."

"Ben, I—" Eden began, tugging at his hand so that he stopped and she could stand in front of him. "Some mistakes can be rectified, some problems can be solved. But there are mistakes, and problems, that simply can't be overcome. I think this is—"

"Eden! Damned if I thought I'd see you out of your office today. Didn't I hear that you were working on closing a big deal with some desert chieftain, or something like that?"

"Holden?" Eden's voice was a near squeak and she looked ready to bolt, to run away from this tall, well-muscled man who looked ready to grab her up in a hug and spin her until she was dizzy.

Ben stepped forward, prepared to intercept the assault, when Eden held out a hand and said, "Holden, big brother and big mouth extraordinare, allow me to present Sheikh Barakah Karif Ramir, the desert chieftain you mentioned just as you were stuffing that size twelve boot in your mouth. Ben, may I present my oldest brother, Holden Fortune."

Ben saw the resemblance then, even if it was limited to Holden Fortune's blue eyes and a certain sameness about his strong, stubborn chin. And he wondered why Eden looked so panicked, as if all she could want from life would be given to her if her brother would disappear in a puff of smoke.

"Mr. Fortune," Ben said, extending his hand in greeting. "It is a pleasure, sir, to meet you. Would you perhaps join us at the sidewalk café we just passed? We could have coffees, and you could tell me all about your lovely sister who has been gracious enough to serve as my guide as I enjoy the pleasures of San Antonio."

Four

Eden didn't know whether she should kick Holden under the table, or just kill him.

For the past ten minutes her brother had been holding court—at Ben's encouragement—telling story after story of Eden's youth.

The time, at age seven, when she forgot to check the cinch on her saddle and ended up sprawled in the dust in the stable yard as her mount raced off toward the open country, the saddle dragging under its belly.

The apology she'd had to write after she'd made ginger cookies with cayenne pepper and their father popped one in his mouth before she could serve them to her intended victims, Holden, and their brother, Logan.

The dress she had sewn in Home Economics class, forgetting to put in the zipper, so that she flunked the course and had to repeat it the next semester.

Still, as Ben laughed, and Holden really got the

bit between his teeth, Eden sat silently, praying he would keep having fun at her expense.

And not ask how she was. How Sawyer was.

But it was inevitable. The conversation finally turned to family, as it always did with the Fortunes.

Holden told her that his wife, Lucinda, seemed to have mastered motherhood as easily as she had every other challenge in her life, then produced a few pictures of his infant daughter, April, passed them over to Ben.

"I carried a beeper with me for weeks before the birth," he told Ben, "half convinced Lucinda would just calmly produce our first child, then simply call me home to meet my child. But, as I said, that's Lucinda. Very competent. She's an OB-GYN, Your Highness. That's doctor of obstetrics and gynecology."

"Yes," Ben answered, smiling. "I am familiar with the term. But I doubt your wife would not have included you in the birth of your child, Holden. There is nothing I can imagine more important than witnessing the birth of one's own child. There cannot be a happier experience for a father. And it would please me if you would call me Ben. I am," he said, smiling at Eden, "playing hooky from my responsibilities at the moment."

Eden sunk another inch on the uncomfortable metal chair, not even bothering to wish herself at the opposite end of the world. Running, wishing. Both were impossible.

If only Holden didn't ask about Sawyer.

"How's Sawyer?" Holden said, showing Eden that she'd been right. Wishing wasn't going to help her.

"Fine, fine," she said quickly; then took a sip of coffee, almost burning her tongue. "And Matthew and Claudia? Has there been any news on their baby?"

She turned to Ben, quickly explaining that her cousin Matt's child, Bryan, had been kidnapped on the day of his christening nearly a year earlier, and had not yet been recovered.

Ben's eyes darkened as he looked from Eden to Holden. "How could such a thing happen? That is, if you are not breaching a family confidence?"

Holden barked out a laugh. "We were served up in the newspapers with everyone's morning coffee the moment word got out about the kidnapping, Ben. I'm not telling any family secrets here. Right, sis?"

Eden nodded and sat back, knowing the story of Bryan had directed attention away from Sawyer. She hated herself for what she'd done, but she couldn't help young Bryan, and she had to protect Sawyer.

"It's the damnedest thing," Holden told Ben, leaning forward, resting his elbows on the glass-topped table. "The christening was at the Double

Crown—that's the family ranch, located southeast of here. Anyway, nobody expected anything but a family party, so no one was really on their guard, although we do have security at the ranch. Bryan was sleeping upstairs one moment, and the next the crib was empty except for the ransom note."

Eden closed her eyes as Holden continued the story that had all the earmarks of a tragedy.

"We recovered the baby. Well," Holden said, grimacing as he looked at Eden, "we recovered *a* baby. But it wasn't Bryan. When footprints were compared, it was made clear to us that Claudia, that's Bryan's mother, was right. This wasn't her child."

"Was not her—but, no, I should not interrupt. Please," Ben said with a wave of his hand, "continue."

Holden picked up his spoon, rubbing it between his fingers. "There wasn't a lot more to be said, not for a long time. Except that amazingly the baby had the hereditary crown-shaped birthmark and rare blood type that proved he was a Fortune, so all the Fortune males had to undergo DNA testing to determine paternity. Obviously, if a female Fortune had been pregnant, the family would've known. Matt and Claudia have taken the mystery baby as their own, even named him Taylor. Their marriage has taken a severe strain and I think that child has been the only thing keeping Claudia sane these last months.

"Until now. Eden," he then added, looking at his sister, "the results of the DNA tests are back. We heard the news this morning. I would have phoned you later, to warn you, but now that you're here..."

Eden's own problems scattered as she took a deep breath, waited for Holden to tell her what he obviously already knew. "Who, Holden?" she asked, dreading his answer. "Who's Taylor's father?"

"Perhaps I will visit that shop I mentioned to you earlier, Eden," Ben said, pushing back his chair and rising to his feet. "This is a family matter, and you should be afforded your privacy. If you will excuse me?"

"Thank you, Ben," Eden said gratefully, watching after him as he strode away, looking every inch the king, even as he blended in with the tourists walking the area with their arms full of plastic shopping bags and video cameras.

"Nice guy," Holden said as Eden looked at her brother once more, willing him to speak, dreading to hear what he might say. "Just think, my little sister on first-name terms with a sheikh. And I think he likes you, sis. Dad would have been over the moon, having a sheikh as a son-in-law."

"And then borrowed money from him immediately after the ceremony," Eden snapped, then felt ashamed of herself. "I'm sorry, Holden. I think my nerves are frazzled now that we've finally gotten everyone to sign on the dotted line. And, for your information, I'm only following my boss's orders, taking Ben sightseeing today. I'll be coming out to the ranch tonight, as a matter of fact, to spend the next two weeks visiting with Mom, trying to unwind. Sawyer and Mrs. Betts are already there."

"Great news, Eden," Holden said, smiling wanly. "We can use all the help at the ranch we can get. I mean, things were bad enough between Claudia and Matt before, but now…Claudia's pretty distraught."

Eden tipped her head to one side, looking at her brother curiously. "About the paternity of the baby, Holden? Why?"

Holden took a deep breath, let it out slowly. "Because, sis, Sheriff Grayhawk said the DNA test reports a ninety-nine point nine percent probability that Taylor is Matt's son."

"*Matt's* son?" Eden collapsed against the back of the chair. "Dear God…"

Eden's brain was still reeling with Holden's news as the limousine pulled up in front of her house on Edgewood Drive, part of a sprawling suburb outside San Antonio. She vaguely remembered giving the address to Haskim, who had given it to the limousine driver before climbing back into the "escort" car that traveled along behind, guarding the Sheikh of Kharmistan.

The sheikh, her own Ben Ramsey, who had been sitting quietly beside her, stroking her hand, allowing her time to regain her composure.

Only now, as she realized that the limousine was no longer moving, did Eden snap to some sort of attention, become aware of her surroundings. Aware of her stupidity.

She remembered the jungle gym in the backyard. The large container of Lego blocks she'd placed at the front door, ready to take to the ranch. Sawyer's colored drawings stuck to the refrigerator door with Mickey Mouse magnets. The pictures of Sawyer that sat on tables in nearly every room. Her house screamed the fact that she didn't live alone. That a child lived with her.

She couldn't let Ben in her house. She simply couldn't.

But how did she keep him out?

She ran a hand through her hair, wincing as she realized that several long dark strands had escaped her French twist to curl beside her face, at her nape. And then, calling on every reserve of strength at her disposal, she smiled.

"I'm so sorry, Ben," she said, extracting her hand from his warm grip. "I've had...I've had such a *shock*..."

"I understand, Eden," Ben told her, stroking a finger down her cheek. "And I am honored that you chose to share your sorrow with me, take me into your confidence. I also understand that you will wish to depart for the family ranch as soon as possible. Holden told me your mother has a home on the ranch, that many of the Fortunes reside on the property. My limousine is at your disposal."

"Oh, no, no, I couldn't do that. Really. I mean, it's wonderful of you to offer, but—"

"Your car is still parked in the city, Eden," Ben pointed out gently. "Haskim will return to your office and make arrangements for it to be delivered either here or to the ranch, if you feel in need of private transportation. But I will not allow you to drive to the Double Crown while you are still so upset."

"You will not *allow?*" Eden felt her temper building, and was grateful to feel her anger, as it was better than her earlier fright, her recent shock. "I don't think you understand, Ben. I'm not asking your permission. I don't have to. I won't."

"Really?" Ben shifted on the seat, looked at her rather indulgently, which angered her even more. "What are you going to do, Eden? How are you going to retrieve your automobile? Please, tell me. I would be very interested to know."

The driver had already opened the door on Eden's

side of the limousine, and she briefly thought about making a break for it, running up the walk, her key in her hand, and then locking the front door behind her.

The thought fled as fast as it had come. Ben was right, she was being stupid, and she had to give in, allow him to help her.

But she still wasn't going to allow Ben inside her house.

"All right, all right," she said, giving an inch so that hopefully she would not be required to give a mile. "If your driver would return in about an hour, I'll be ready to go."

"Such a gracious acceptance of my offer of assistance. Is that an example of Texas hospitality, Eden? If so, may I suggest that you amend your statement to include the fact that I will be accompanying you to the Fortune ranch for dinner. At the express invitation of your brother, as a matter of fact."

"Holden invited you to the ranch? Why? Where was I when this was happening?"

"He invited me because I expressed an interest in locating some more diverse stock for my stables and he believes I could satisfy my wishes at the Double Crown. As for the where of it? You were sitting across from us at the table, Eden, very much in shock and lost inside your own thoughts, I am afraid. Which, again, is why I cannot allow you to drive yourself to the ranch. Now, Eden, perhaps you will be so gracious as to invite me into your house while you pack your suitcases?''

''I—I can't…that is, the place is a mess. I mean, the housekeeper is…she's having minor surgery this week, and I've been working such long hours over the oil and gas deal. The house is a shambles. A shambles, really. I couldn't invite you in.''

''Eden,'' Ben said firmly, ''I am beginning to believe you are trying to get rid of me. I thought we had gotten beyond our misunderstandings of the past. Can you really not forgive me? Can you refuse my offer of friendship, even if I have rashly frightened you with my hopes for something deeper than friendship?''

Eden looked to the open door, to the driver patiently standing outside, pretending not to listen to their conversation. ''I must be losing my mind,'' she said, dropping her head into her hands, admitting defeat. ''Give me ten minutes, Ben, to pick up the worst of it, and then you can come in, all right?''

He lifted her hand to his mouth, pressed a kiss in her palm. ''Thank you, Eden,'' he said simply. She quickly exited the limousine, fearful that she would throw herself into his arms, beg for his comfort.

His understanding. His forgiveness.

His love?

Her hands trembling, Eden searched in her handbag for her keys, then wasted precious moments trying to fit the key in the dead bolt.

Once inside, she flattened herself against the closed door, took several deep breaths, then began her race through the house, picking up Lego construction toys and pictures and a purple stuffed dinosaur.

She removed a dozen Disney videos from the open cabinet in the family room and stuffed them beneath one of the couches.

A drawing of she and Sawyer holding Easter baskets was slammed inside the refrigerator, along with a list of telephone numbers for backup baby-sitters and Sawyer's play school schedule for April and May.

It was all she could do, besides quickly closing all the drapes at the back of the house to hide the existence of the jungle gym and Sawyer's small tricycle that sat beside the bright green covered sandbox in the shape of a turtle.

She made one last sweep through the downstairs of the two-story Colonial, then skidded to a halt in the flagstone foyer once more, catching a glimpse of herself in the mirror above the hall table.

She looked like a wild woman, her eyes wide, her cheeks pale as a white cotton sheet, her hair all but tumbling free of the French twist after her run-in with the sofa skirt.

She nearly jumped out of her shoes when the doorbell rang and she could see Ben standing on the front porch, the outline of his body visible through the narrow window at the side of the front door.

Taking yet another deep breath—she felt as if she'd just run a record marathon—she threw open the door and plastered a smile on her face. "Thanks for indulging me, Ben. Come on in. You can wait for me in the living room. Can I get you something to drink?"

She winced inwardly at her last statement, knowing she'd gone too far. Because she had already been planning to go to her mother's on Friday evening, the refrigerator was nearly empty. The only thing she could offer him besides ice water was a juice drink in a paper carton with the picture of a cartoon character on it.

"I would not wish to inconvenience you further," Ben said, walking into the living room, looking toward the formal dining room that was visible to the left and rear of the house. "You have a lovely home, Eden. It is very much like you. Cool, well-ordered, and yet with whispers of whimsy. Quite wonderfully female."

"Um...okay," Eden said, wondering when she

had lost the ability to articulate anything other than a few stupidly betraying words at a time.

"However, if you do not mind, I would ask that I be allowed to turn on the television, which I do not see in this lovely room. I have this fascination with CNN, you understand. Besides," he added, "the Yankees played a late game last night out in California, so I have not yet been able to locate the score."

"The...the *Yankees?* You follow the Yankees?"

"Do not look so amazed, Eden," he said, following her as she retraced her steps through the foyer, heading for the kitchen, and the family room that lay beyond it. "I developed a love of the game while at Yale. As a matter of fact, I still play second base in a small league I began in Kharmistan. Haskim is our right fielder, and we play against at least a dozen other teams in our league. I do not believe there is a schoolchild in Kharmistan who does not own a bat and a mitt—and a Mark McGwire baseball card. Do not look so shocked, Eden. Did you think our only form of recreation had something to do with racing camels across the desert?"

Eden stopped just inside the kitchen, leaned against the wall, covering her eyes with her hand, and began to laugh. That laughter started out small, but it grew quickly, until she knew she would have fallen down if she hadn't been leaning against the wall.

She laughed until her shoulders shook. She laughed until tears streamed down her face. She laughed until she knew she was about to dissolve into tears if she didn't stop, immediately.

"I think I'm hysterical," she admitted when she could finally get herself back under control. "I know Kharmistan is very westernized, if that is the proper term. I know you have modern cities, museums, theaters, universities. In my mind, I know this. And yet every time I think of Kharmistan, all I can think of are sand, tents, oil fields, and women wearing veils to go out on the street. I certainly don't think about baseball cards. What an idiot I am, Ben. I think I'm laughing because otherwise I'd just cry, I'm that ashamed of myself."

"Kharmistan women have not worn the veil in two generations, Eden. And Lord help the man who would try to make them go back to the old ways. Or did I not make myself clear? Perhaps this will help. Haskim's sister, Fadilah, is our first-string catcher. She can throw out a man trying for second without coming up off her knees."

That did it. Eden looked at Ben for long moments, then stumbled across the kitchen and fell into a chair. "As I said, I'm an idiot. You're not the stereotype, Ben, *I* am. Prejudging, typecasting, and more than willing to believe that Kharmistan is still existing in another century. Backward. Undemocratic. A militaristic state. Except you're all busy collecting baseball cards and my research told me that the average income of your subjects would put them in our second-highest income tax bracket.''

"My people do not pay income tax, Eden," Ben told her, walking past her and into the family room, picking up the remote control that sat on the arm of one of the couches and turning on the television. "There is no poverty, very little crime, and our largest problem right now is finding enough television satellite dishes to supply the needs of all of our people."

"And your subjects look to you as the creator of all their good fortune, don't they? You're sitting pretty, as the saying goes."

Ben was flipping through the channels with the expertise of a gifted channel surfer. "I only continue what my grandfather began, the reforms my father implemented. The world moves, as my father told me, and only a fool chooses to fall off rather than to move with it. I look forward to the day the Sheikh of Kharmistan is little more than a figurehead, much like the kings and queens of England, with our own form of parliament for the most part making and interpreting the laws of our land. Not that I am planning to abdicate, of course. But my sons will continue the progress that has been made, leading our people into the future you and I and the entire world populace dream about now, as we enter the twenty-first century.''

"Your sons. Of course,'' Eden said, her head spinning with all the contradictions that confused her even as Ben unwittingly enlightened her, told her what her son's future could be, would be, if she were to tell Ben of Sawyer's existence.

She stood very still for a few moments, trying to get over her embarrassment at having so lost her composure, trying to form the words she knew she must now say.

"Ben, I'm sorry. I'm really sorry. I've been insulting, perhaps even condescending—and I've betrayed myself as being shamefully ignorant in an area I should have familiarized myself with thoroughly before you even arrived in Texas. Mostly, I'm angry with myself for falling apart after Holden told me about young Taylor, about Matt. We've had a horrible year at the ranch, ever since little Bryan was kidnapped. I think everything is beginning to catch up with me, make me stupid. Clumsy.''

Ben clicked off the television and turned to look at her. He didn't approach her physically, but she could feel the pull of him, the strong physical attraction he must know she felt. ''And my unexpected reappearance in your life, Eden? That has not helped you, has it? You have been very kind, if reluctantly welcoming, and I believe you have begun to relax in my company, if only for short, quite enjoyable spaces of time. But I frighten you, for reasons I am aware of, for reasons I sense but cannot know."

"No," Eden protested weakly, backing up a step, even as he remained a good fifteen feet away from her. "I'm not afraid of you, Ben."

"It is still the early days in our renewed association, Eden," Ben said quietly. "You are confused, caught off your guard, as I was not, since I have been planning our meeting for six long months. You have your life here in Texas to consider, your large family and its considerable problems. I cannot blame you for anything you might say or do right now. And yet, Eden, I must tell you that I do not appreciate untruths, however kindly they may be intentioned. But I will give you time, Eden, if not space, in which to come to terms with both your anger over our wasted years and my hopes for our combined future."

And then, not waiting for her answer, he turned back to the television and clicked it on, just as if he hadn't said anything more than to perhaps comment on the weather.

Arrogant man! Yet he'd reminded her so much of how Sawyer had looked, responded, last week at the mall when he had told her he thanked her very much, but he was entirely too grown up to need her to accompany him to the bathroom.

Eden had felt herself being kindly, gently but firmly put in her place then, and she felt much the same way now. There was something about the tone of voice, the indulgent tilt of the head, the calm assurance, that had impressed her when her son had asserted himself, that impacted on her now when Ben forthrightly stated his concerns, his plans for their future.

Sawyer she could overrule, and had overruled that day at the mall as she took his hand and led him, protesting, to the ladies' room.

But his father?

Eden knew she could say no to a sheikh. She could say no to a president, a king. But say no to Ben—and really mean it?

Say no to this man who had haunted her dreams for nearly six years?

Say no to this man who had given her the great gift of her wonderful son even as she had thought she'd lost him, lost his love?

Say no to this man who had unexpectedly reappeared just when it seemed she needed his strength and comfort most, begging her indulgence, broadly hinting that he wanted her back in his life. For now. For forever.

Eden knew she wouldn't know where to begin to say no to this man.

"O-okay...well..." Eden stammered at last, staring at Ben's back as he surfed through the channels with typical male expertise, acting as if he had forgotten her presence. "I—I guess I'll run upstairs and throw some clothing into a suitcase. I won't need much more than a few things, as I keep my ranch clothes at my mom's anyway."

He nodded without turning around. "Very good, Eden. There's no rush. Ah, word of our agreement this morning already has made the business news, I see. Nadim will be pleased."

"Yeah, right. Good for Nadim," Eden said, then all but ran out of the room, not wanting to leave Ben alone in her house any longer than necessary. She picked up a toy sheriff's badge that had somehow found its way into the bowl on the kitchen table, stuffed it into her pocket, and went upstairs to pack.

To pack, and to phone her mother, beg her to warn everyone that Ben was bringing her out to the ranch. Beg her mother to keep Sawyer hidden while Eden had Ben deliver her to her Uncle Ryan's house instead of her mother's. Beg her to please, please, for God's sake, please warn everyone to keep their mouths shut and all without telling them why!

If Ben had to be told about Sawyer, and Eden

knew in her heart that she couldn't keep the news from him much longer and still be able to live with herself, she would have to plan that conversation carefully. She would likewise have to prepare Sawyer, and plan his meeting with his father with the utmost care.

Ben hated "untruths." Anything longer than another day of delay would make any confession too late, would brand her as someone who had not been prepared to tell the truth, someone who might have decided not to speak at all.

But the consequences to herself were not important, her own future was no longer important...and probably already beyond her control. She had to think of the boy, the man. First and foremost, she had to think of Sawyer, of Ben. She could not let father and son meet accidentally, without either of them being prepared, forewarned.

The drive to the Double Crown took forever...if forever lasted about an hour and was spent traveling over beautiful open country Eden had loved for all of her life.

Not that she had taken time to look at the scenery. Instead, she had filled Ben in on the news Holden had told her, as everyone at the ranch was bound to still be upset, and perhaps not as ready for company as Holden had thought they might be.

She lowered the window when they reached the new security station at the entrance to the long road leading onto the ranch, identified herself to the guard, then sat back as the limousine passed through the gates.

"That reminds me," Ben said as he looked at the guard who was holding open the gate, "I never did order those hats, did I? Although I must say the guard looks much more complete in jeans and vest than Haskim would look in his *kibr* and a ten-gallon cowboy hat on his head."

"That's true enough," Eden said, knowing Ben was trying to lighten her mood, and more than happy to go along. "You might want to rethink that purchase, or buy some jeans and boots, and a few other *cowboy* accessories."

Ben looked at her, one dark eyebrow raised expressively. "You think I am mocking this typical Western costume, Eden?"

"No, I think you're a man with deep pockets and a rather delicious sense of humor. Or am I wrong, and it wasn't you who said you'd decided to buy Nadim a Mexican sombrero—one of those made especially for tourists, a mile wide and covered in fancy designs and sequins?"

"The man could do with some loosening up, Eden," Ben said, trying to be serious but then smiling as Eden shook her head at him.

"Ah, thank you, Ben," she said for what seemed like the hundredth time in the hour since they'd left her house on Edgewood Drive. "You were right, much as I hate to admit it. I probably would have run off the road if I'd tried to drive out here by myself. As it is, my stomach is still full of butterflies. Thank you for the ride, and most definitely for the company. Although I still don't have the faintest idea what I'm going to say to Claudia. Or Matt, for that matter. Right now, I'm thinking about stringing him up from the strongest beam in the barn."

"May I make a suggestion, Eden?"

She sighed. "Ben, at this point, knowing I have to go see Claudia, talk to her, I think I'd be crazy not to get all the advice I can find."

"In that case, may I *advise* that you should meet with your cousin Matt first, before you see his wife, and then listen more than you speak. There may be some explanation for the test results."

"Oh, really? Like what, Ben?"

He shook his head. "I have no idea, Eden. I simply do not wish to see you jump to any rash conclusions that might end with hurt feelings between you and your cousin."

Eden stared out the window of the limousine, seeing her Uncle Ryan's home—the original ranch house—as they rounded a turn in the road. Its sand-colored adobe walls offered welcome, offered respite, reminded her of the simplicity of life long ago, when the original builders had first settled here.

What must this old house be thinking about the events of the past year? If the walls could talk, what would they say?

The original house had been added to over the years, growing along with the Fortune family, until it was a huge, impressive structure, but it still retained that simplicity of design, that promise of peace and safety. Eden had played in the massive inner courtyard as a child, played with her brothers and cousins, laughed with them, dreamed silly dreams with them.

"It's a shame we have to grow up, isn't it, Ben?" she said as she realized she'd been silent too long. "How much less complicated life was when we were children. I think my largest problem was whether or not Logan and Matt would let me tag along when they exercised their horses. Now we're grown up, or at least we hope so, and there's another generation here at the ranch. My brother Logan, once the Great Playboy of the Western World, has got himself a wife, and a child he hadn't known existed until a few months ago, and Holden and Lucinda are new parents, as well. My cousin Vanessa has married the FBI agent who came to investigate Bryan's kidnapping—and who nearly got himself killed in the process. If I know Vanessa, she won't settle for less than a half dozen babies of her own. Matt's son has been kidnapped, the infant he and Claudia took in has turned out to be his natural son, and I...and I..."

"And you, Eden?" Ben prompted when she bit her lip, shook her head.

"Nothing," she said, dredging up a smile from somewhere deep inside her. "I'm just tired, that's all. And you're right, Ben. I'll see Matt first, let him tell me whatever he wants to tell me."

She sighed as the limousine eased to a stop in front of her uncle's ranch house. "And then I'll kill him. Ah, here's Holden, already coming to meet us. Or *you*, I should say. I hope you meant it when you said you wanted to see some horses, because if I know my brother, you're going to see a bunch of them in the next hour."

And you won't see Sawyer at all, not yet, she concluded silently as Holden pulled open the door, giving her a look that told her she, too, was going to be seeing a lot of her brother later this evening. A look that told her while she might be here to talk to Matt she'd also be doing a lot of explaining of her own—after Ben had gone back to San Antonio.

Five

The stars shone brightly in the Texas night sky, nearly as clear and shining as those over the skies of Kharmistan, taking Ben back to memories of trips into the desert with his father years ago.

They would sleep under the stars, throwing off all the outward trappings of sheikh and royal heir, returning to the real life that would always be a part of their mostly desert country. Feeling that nomadic blood stirring, breathing in the honey-heavy air of old dreams, new freedoms.

Ben's father had felt the twice-yearly trips necessary, and it was only coincidental that they were also enjoyable, and now held some of Ben's fondest memories of the man, of the country they both loved. The land they and their forbearers held in their hands, land they ruled and were ruled by, land that was their past and held their future.

A man, a horse, a few homely essentials. That was the way to remember who you were, why you were where fate had placed you.

Ben sensed that Texans felt the same feelings, the

same stirrings, the same past that mingled with the future. He felt sure that the man standing beside him now, sipping coffee from a huge mug, had more in common with Sheikh Barakah Karif Ramir than he would believe possible.

He sensed that Holden, like his brother, his cousins, would want to take him apart, piece by piece, if they knew he had loved Eden in Paris and then left her.

And he would not blame them.

Which only made him like these Fortunes even more. They were family. Strong family. The bonds were solid, the roots ran deep. Eden had grown in fertile soil.

The silence grew, soft and companionable above the occasional faint whinny from the stables, the harsh cries of night birds on the hunt, the chatter of crickets. The air smelled of horse, of sweet hay, of wildflowers sleeping in the night.

The sounds were different, the smells were different from his homeland. But the mood was the same. Comfortable. Somehow powerful. The heady aphrodisiac of sturdy land under your feet, the wide sky above. Land that was always there, would always be there. Sky that promised the limitless boundaries of eternity.

Ben took another sip from his coffee mug, then turned to look at Holden. "It is good to be alive, is it not? For all the trials, the turmoil, the heartaches. For all the worries, both small and global, for all the responsibilities we bear, all the disappointments we must face, it is good to be alive. If only to stand here on a night like this and let sweet peace and simple hope embrace us.''

Holden spilled the dregs of coffee from his cup with a sharp swing of his arm, then shook his head at Ben, smiled. "No wonder Lucinda took me aside after dinner tonight to tell me she thought you were a cross between Pierce Brosnan—her favorite movie star—and her much adored grandfather. My wife is of Native American descent, you know. Her grandfather was, to hear her tell it, a grand old man with a sacred love of the land and a healthy respect for nature, the simpler things most of us are usually too pressured to even notice.''

Ben emptied his own cup into the stable yard, and turned to lean against the five-barred gate, his elbows on the top bar. "I will consider this a very great compliment, to be compared to her revered grandfather—although I do not think I shall comment on her more fanciful statement.''

Holden shrugged, grinned. "Hey, what can I say? She's a new mother. I learned a long time ago not to argue with anyone's mama.''

"You have, I believe, just shown yourself to also be a very wise man, like your wife's grandfather.

Do you mind if I tell you something I learned years ago? I read that it was proposed by William Penn, who first settled your Pennsylvania, I believe, that the American Indian is in fact descended from the original tribes of Israel. He compared the skin tone, the high-bridged noses, the general countenance, stature and body shape, even some similar customs, and concluded that your wife's forbearers had migrated West through Asia, crossed a now disappeared land bridge to Alaska, and then settled in various parts of North America. There are even ancient Indian legends that seem to support Penn's suppositions. In all, it remains an interesting theory, that we possibly were once all the same people.''

''That it does,'' Holden answered, petting the soft velvet nose of a horse that had ambled over to the fence. ''There's also a theory that Japanese sailed to the East long centuries before the Spanish conquest and integrated with the Quechuan, Incan populations in highland Peru. But don't take that as a history lesson, because I could be wrong on most of it, okay?''

Ben's smile was warm, thoughtful. ''Do you ever think, Holden, that if we trace our history and our hearts, that we truly are all one people? Or perhaps we do believe that, and still persist in behaving like children, fighting with our siblings.''

The horse moved away, and Holden sighed,

watching the animal before he blended back into the night. "I can't thank you enough for being here this evening, Ben. Just in case you didn't know that I invited you here for another reason besides showing off the Double Crown horses. I thought we needed a neutral party here tonight, to take some of the edge off the news we received this morning."

"I am happy I could be of service. About your cousin, Matthew," Ben added, nodding, "I am sure you must all be in some sort of shock. I know I was rather worried about Eden for a while, although she seemed happier after speaking with your cousin. Less shocked, more worried. I am not sure, however, which I prefer her to be."

"It's Matt's explanation, Ben," Holden said as they both moved away from the fence, started back toward the lights from the house. "It sounds like something out of a soap opera. He's Taylor's father, but the only way he could be—according to him— is if someone somehow got hold of the donation he made to a sperm bank in California years ago, when he was a medical student there. He didn't do it for the money, like many medical students do, but because he believed medical technology is meant to help create life for those who could not otherwise hope to hold a child in their arms. Idealistic, I agree, but that's how he felt.

"He swears on his mother's grave that he's been

faithful to Claudia from the day they met, and I believe him. Hell, I've never seen a man so upset, so totally at sea. I mean, they both love Taylor with all their hearts, and really want to raise him...but none of us could have been prepared to hear that the child is really Matt's son. But my Uncle Ryan is standing by his son, and so am I. We all are. Sheriff Grayhawk is going to investigate this sperm bank lead in an effort to get to the bottom of this.''

Ben nodded, understanding easily. ''Family is family. There is no greater bond.'' He looked toward the house, saw the figure standing on the porch. ''Ah, I believe my keen desert eyes see Mr. Ryan Fortune waiting for us, Holden. Shall we join him?''

Holden laughed, and Ben saw that his small joke had further relaxed the man, which had been his intention. There had been too much tension stretching in the air since he arrived at the ranch, even more tension than he believed could be caused by today's development with Matthew Fortune. So he assumed that his presence was, perhaps, a little intimidating.

And he had not liked the way everyone had looked at Eden when they entered the house, their eyes more full of questions than clouded by the dilemma of Matthew and young Taylor.

In fact, Ryan Fortune, Eden's uncle, and definitely the patriarch of the Fortune tribe, had eyed him as closely as Nadim watched the ambitious Minister of Public Funds. The scrutiny had almost made Ben feel guilty, as if he had committed some crime, one of which he was not yet aware. One he could be punished for at any moment. Punished for, and then banished.

Yet Ryan Fortune was all smiles when they reached him on the porch, telling Ben again how grateful he was that he had brought his niece to the Double Crown.

"Eden is with Claudia now, and they're having a woman-to-woman talk, I believe. Eden has always been very good with that sort of thing. If she hadn't gone into law, I believe she might have made a fine diplomat. However, as she's probably going to be with Claudia for some time, she asked that I say her good-nights for her," Ryan said.

Ben was familiar with the term "bum's rush," and he was pretty sure he was suddenly close to the "Here's your hat, what's your hurry" speech.

"Uncle Ryan?" Holden said, seemingly caught between surprise and embarrassment. "It's only nine o'clock. Surely you aren't saying Ben should leave already?"

"No, of course not," Ryan Fortune said, looking at his nephew with an intensity that probably had the man wondering if he had a coffee stain on the front of his white shirt. "It's just that we've had a problem at the *saw*mill, Holden. Somebody forgot to latch something or other, and somehow logs have…have *escaped*. I think you might want to get on the horn, contact the manager up there and ʼfind out the extent of the damage before something *else* happens and things get *worse*."

Holden stood very still for a moment, his eyes shifting from side to side, then said quickly, "Of course, of course. I'll get right on it, Uncle Ryan. Ben," he then said, turning to extend his hand to Ben, who kept his face carefully emotionless, "I hate to rush away like this, but I do have to take care of this. Uncle Ryan will make sure you and your staff know the way back to San Antonio. Although we'd all be pleased to have you visit again soon, if you can manage to include us in your schedule."

"I am sure that would be possible, Holden, especially as you have promised me a day-long ride around this fine property. As it is, I should be getting back to the hotel. Nadim, my advisor, will be keeping a light on, you understand, pacing and worrying like an old hen with one chick. That amuses me, but I cannot soothe my conscience with the thought that he deserves a little worry from time to time."

Within five minutes, the assembled Fortunes had said their good-nights and Ben found himself back in his limousine, the driver making his way slowly over the dark, twisting road that led back to the main gates. He lowered the side window, reluctant to leave the smells of grassland and meadows, wondering if Eden truly had been too involved with her cousin's wife to personally bid him good-night.

There was something going on at the Fortune ranch. Something that included Matthew Fortune's new problem, but it was not limited to that problem. Ben had been raised to scent out intrigue, and there had been intrigue aplenty tonight, easily sniffed out over the aroma of fine food, over the lush smells of the night.

Somewhere, deep inside himself, he could not dismiss the niggling feeling that *he* had something to do with that air of intrigue, of nervousness, of a secret not meant to be shared.

The limousine came to a gentle stop and the glass divider between Ben and the hired American driver slid down. "Yes?" Ben asked, leaning forward, trying to look past the limousine's headlights. "Is there something wrong? An animal on the road?"

"No, sir," the driver said as Ben heard car doors closing behind him and Haskim opened the back door of the limousine, poked his head inside to check on his prince.

"Not an animal," the driver went on. "A child. I caught a glimpse of him as the headlights hit the side of the road when we turned that last corner.

Over there, sir, in that small clump of brush. I think he's hiding out.''

"A child? Are you sure? It is past nine o'clock, and dark. What would a child be doing out here this late at night? Haskim, you will approach the child, slowly and carefully, so as not to frighten it, and bring it to me. No, wait, I will go with you. After all, it is not as if I cannot do things for myself.''

"I'll back up a little once you get out, sir,'' the driver said. "That way the headlights will make it easier for you to see him if he tries to run away. That's what's wrong with the world today, sir, you know. Parents letting little kids run wild, all times of the day and night. The child didn't look to be any taller than my boy, Sam Houston, and he's only seven. You get him, sir, and we'll put a little fear into him, teach him not to go running wild.''

"Yes, thank you,'' Ben said, rolling his eyes as he looked up at Haskim, then levered himself out of the limousine, stepping into the tall grass beside the roadway, allowing Haskim to lead the way forward, toward the clump of what the American driver had called brush.

"I hope the child knows his name, Haskim,'' he said as they walked along, trying to see in the dim light of the headlights. "There must be dozens of families living within the large confines of this splendid ranch. Now, go slowly, Haskim. We do not want him to bolt and try to escape us, for he could be hurt running into the darkness.''

"Yes, Your Highness,'' Haskim answered, holding his right hand quite near his hip.

Ben took hold of his left elbow and pulled him to a halt. "Haskim, I am assuming that there is a pistol beneath your *kibr,* am I right? And if I am, do you seriously believe it will be necessary to protect your prince by shooting a young boy?''

"No, Your Highness,'' Haskim said, bowing his head. "I am ashamed, Your Highness, and beg your forgiveness.''

"Granted,'' Ben said, grinning. "Unless the *kid* shoots me, of course.''

"Your Highness?''

"Oh, relax, Haskim. I think you are watching too many American television shows. Not everyone in America carries a weapon. Now, stay here. I think I see him. He may be less frightened by my presence if you and your *kibr* and *kaffiyeh* are not so much in evidence. You look like Casper's cousin, the Not So Friendly Ghost, standing out here.''

"Your Highness?''

Leaving Haskim where he stood, a bright white beacon of flowing cotton in a dark night, Ben slowly approached the clump of brush, holding out his hand, a smile on his face. "Do not be afraid, little one. I mean no harm. Come, I will take you home.''

"I'm never afraid," a small voice answered him. "And if I want to go home, I know how. I came out to see my mom, who's still up at the main house, even though she knows it's bedtime and she has to tuck me in. So," the small voice continued, with just the hint of apprehension finally coloring the quite grown-up confidence he had been articulating, "you can go away now."

"But *I* am afraid," Ben answered, taking a few more careful steps toward the small, dark outline visible between the twisting branches of brush. "I am afraid that I have lost my way, and I would only hope that you might help me find the home of Mr. Ryan Fortune, who I am to see tonight. Can you help me, as it would seem you know your way around this great ranch?"

"Uncle Ryan?" The voice had regained its strength. "You're here to see Uncle Ryan? Then why are you going the wrong way? The ranch house is behind you. That's a limousine, isn't it? I've never been in one of those. My friend, Randy, he comes to play school in one every day. Mom says his parents spoil him, but I think it would be neat to ride in a limousine. Do you like it?"

"I like it very much," Ben answered, taking two more steps and then stopping in the middle of the road, where the headlights could show his form, a bit of his expression. If he did not look like a bad man, perhaps the boy would begin to trust him. "Would you like to sit up front with my driver, and tell him how to find the ranch house? He will even let you wear his cap, if you want."

"Mom says I'm not supposed to get in strange cars, or talk to strange people. That's dangerous. So you hafta go away now, okay?"

Ben sighed, running a hand through his hair. The boy was right. He should not talk to strangers, accept rides in strange cars. The mother had taught the child well, even if she did not seem able to keep him where he was put. "Haskim," he said so that the servant rushed up to him, bowed. "Get back in your car and return to the ranch house. Bring Mr. Holden Fortune to me. Do you know Mr. Holden Fortune, young man?" he asked, calling to the child.

"Uncle Holden?"

"Ah. Did you hear that, Haskim? It is now doubly definite. We have discovered a Fortune child wandering the ranch in the darkness. Well, with all that is transpiring here today, it is no surprise a small child was allowed to misplace himself, is it? Go on, Haskim, ask Mr. Fortune if he will be kind enough to come retrieve his nephew while the boy and I broaden our acquaintance."

"But, Your Highness. For you to stand out here, unprotected—"

"Haskim, I am not going to leave this child. You

know, there's something to be said about absolute rule and a healthy fear of incurring the wrath of one's prince. Would you care to have me consider that, Haskim?''

Ben smiled as the servant bowed three times, then quickly sprinted back to the car. A moment later the car was backing into the field alongside the roadway, then returning to the ranch house.

''Are you a king?''

Ben turned back to look where the boy had been, still straining to see him through the darkness. He saw that the boy had stepped slightly away from the brush, so that he could see that the child was indeed a young boy, and with the posture of a strong young warrior, perhaps a bit of a prince himself.

''A king? Perhaps. In my country, I am the sheikh. Sheikh Barakah Karif Ramir of Kharmistan, if you want to hear the whole of it. But I would be best pleased if you were to call me Ben. Will you do that? And I might then call you…?''

The shadowy figure took another step forward, moved into the light of the headlamps on the limousine. ''Sawyer,'' he said, holding his chin high, his dark eyes staring straight into Ben's. ''You can call me Sawyer.''

All Ben could do was stare. To look at this young boy. This Sawyer Fortune.

This boy who looked at him with his own eyes.

"Who is your mother, Sawyer?" he heard himself ask, knowing his voice was little more than a rough rasp, that he was probably frightening the boy. "That is…" he amended, trying to gather his shattered thoughts, trying to slow his heartbeat that pounded as if he had just run a long race, only to fall into the dust a foot before the finish line. "Perhaps I know her? I have met a few of your family members, you see, so I am curious. Is your mother's name Eden?"

"You look funny," Sawyer said, backing up a few steps. "Sort of mad, and maybe a little bit sick. Are you sick? And why do you sound so funny? Like you're trying not to shout at me?"

Ben turned his head, wiped a hand across his mouth, turned to face the boy once more. He could not be right. He had to control himself. Eden would not do such a thing to him. She would not have hidden his son from him. She was not a mean person, a spiteful person. There had to be some mistake.

"I am sorry, Sawyer. I did not mean to frighten you. I—I was only surprised to see that you are such an intelligent-looking young man, and yet you have allowed yourself to be lost in the dark, just like a baby."

"I'm not lost, and I'm *not* a baby!" Sawyer exclaimed, stamping his foot in the dirt. "And I don't like you."

Ben let out his breath in a small rush, knowing he had at least diverted Sawyer from thinking he might be ill, or worse. Even if he did feel sick at heart, devastated by a knowledge that he was a fool, had always been a fool, and that Eden must hate him with all of her being.

Hate him, and fear him. Fear him very much.

He became aware of the sound of vehicles all but skidding to a stop on the roadway, the sound of car doors slamming shut, the voice of Holden Fortune calling to his young nephew as he ran along the roadway, past the limousine, to stop just beside Ben.

"Ben?" Holden asked, looking at him. Ben refused to turn, to take his fevered gaze away from Sawyer, to look at his new friend and see the truth in his eyes. "Oh, brother. You know, don't you? Yes, of course you do. He's the spitting image of you, which I might have realized sooner, if I'd had any reason to suspect...if Eden had confided in any of us before tonight. Are...are you all right?"

"I believe a house as large as your uncle's contains sufficient guest rooms for Haskim and myself," he heard himself say. "Have two such rooms prepared by tomorrow morning, and expect my arrival no later than ten o'clock. I, in turn, will expect Eden to be waiting for me, prepared to answer any questions I might have. Is that clear?"

"Now, look, Ben..." Holden began as Sawyer

ran up to his uncle, flung his arms around Holden's knees. "Oh, hell, I'm not even going to try to lie to you now. What would be the point? It would take a blind man to not notice the resemblance, and an idiot not to be able to count on his fingers and figure out the rest of it. I'll have Eden waiting for you at her mother's house tomorrow morning, although Sawyer won't be there. You can understand why not, Ben, I'm sure. Someone at the front gate will direct your driver, all right?"

"Thank you," Ben said stiffly, still staring at the spot where he had first seen Sawyer, holding on to the moment he had realized that he had a son. He had a son! "And now, if you will excuse me, the hour grows late and I have much to do."

"There's an explanation, you know. A perfectly reasonable explanation—*Mr. Ramsey*," Holden called after him as Ben turned and his long strides took him back to the open door of the limousine. "Don't forget that!"

"Your Highness?" Haskim did not look at Ben as he held open the door to the limousine. He was far too occupied with gawking at Sawyer Fortune, who was now skipping alongside his uncle, heading back to the Jeep he'd driven in, having chosen to follow Haskim's car. "That boy, Your Highness. Did you see him?"

"Yes, Haskim, I have seen him," Ben said,

climbing into the limousine, collapsing against the soft leather cushions. "You have seen him. But Nadim has not. No others have seen him. To Nadim, to everyone else, the child does not exist. Do you understand?"

"I understand, Your Highness," Haskim said, bowing. "I serve my prince. I live to serve any royal prince of Kharmistan with the blood of your father and his father in his veins."

"Thank you, Haskim," Ben said, lowering his head into his hands as the door closed and the driver pulled forward once more.

Ben sat quietly for a long time, trying to control his thoughts, trying to reconcile his nearly overwhelming anger with his own bone-deep guilt.

Then he touched the button that raised the glass between driver and passenger, and pulled his cell phone and small electronic notebook from his jacket pocket. He had a lot of calls to make, a raft of different orders to set into motion before he returned to the Double Crown the next morning.

The first call to an agency in New York would have a discreet watch put on the Double Crown ranch within the hour, so that no one could come or go—whether by car or by plane or even by helicopter—without the knowledge of Barakah Karif Ramir, Sheikh of Kharmistan.

Especially one lying, deceitful young woman, or one very small, infinitely precious boy.

There were three voice mail messages from Eden waiting for Ben by the time he returned to the Palace Lights hotel in San Antonio. Stripping off his shirt, he tossed it to the floor, vowing never to wear it, or his blue slacks, ever again. He pushed the button and the first of those messages played over the speakerphone.

"Ben? Oh, God, Ben! I know you're not there yet. You just left, and Holden told me how upset you looked. And I don't blame you, Ben. I can't blame you. But you have to believe me—it wasn't supposed to happen this way. I was going to tell you. Tomorrow. I was still trying to find the words, the moment. You can understand that, can't you? Call me. Please call me!"

He glared at the phone, shook his head, waited for the second message.

"Ben? I suppose you're not back yet. If you are, please call me. I want to apologize again. Apologize forever, if that's what it takes. But I couldn't tell you, not yet. All I could think about was Sawyer. *He* had to be told, before I could say anything to you. I have to prepare him, break the news to him slowly.... Oh, Ben! Call me, call me as soon as you get in!"

"Prepare him? Break the news to him slowly?" Ben glared at the telephone as he took off his shoes, stripped out of his slacks and underwear. "Yes, I can see the wisdom in that. But did you think about my reaction, Eden? Or did my feelings not hold any concern for you?"

The last message was short, and Eden's voice was stronger now, more in control. "You and I will meet at my mother's tomorrow at ten. Sawyer will be with Holden, who has agreed to take care of him until you and I can come to some sort of agreement. If you don't agree with this, if you make any attempt to see Sawyer outside my presence, I will make sure you never see him again. Do you understand that, Ben? I know I hurt you, and I'm sorry. But I will not allow anything, or anyone, to hurt my son. Not even his father. Now, good night!"

Not even his father? *Never* his father! Ben would allow his eyes to be plucked out before he could think to hurt his own son. Did Eden not understand that? Had she forgotten so much? Did she know him so little?

Ben carefully erased the messages, grateful that Nadim was still out, still enjoying his dinner with the members of the American triad, basking in his success. If Nadim had been here in the suite, if he had picked up the phone when Eden called...

No. Ben would not think about that. It was

enough that he knew Nadim could not know about Sawyer's existence. Not until Ben had taken steps to protect the child, insure his future, present him to the people of Kharmistan as his son and heir.

Kharmistan was a nation at peace, a nation that had been at peace for long decades. A nation that harbored no real rebels, no prospect of revolution. But it was also the same nation that was the home of Yusuf Nadim, cousin to the sheikh, father-in-law and powerful chief advisor to the sheikh, a man who had thought to see his own grandson on the throne of Kharmistan.

Nadim would not be happy to learn of Sawyer's existence. He might even try to rally some sort of support behind the notion that his prince was immoral, unfit to rule, having fathered an illegitimate child he was now thrusting at the heads of his people, proclaiming him heir.

No. Nadim could not know. Not yet. Not until Ben found a way to explain Sawyer to his people, explain Eden to his people. Because he would give up the throne before he would give up his son. And he would marry Eden Fortune, make her his wife in the eyes of his God and his people, take her to Kharmistan as his father had taken his mother there thirty years ago.

He would marry Eden. For the boy. And because he loved her, had always loved her, would always love her. Even now, when he was so angry with her that he had to leave the Double Crown Ranch tonight without confronting her.

And if she would not have him? If she refused to take Sawyer to Kharmistan, have the three of them start a new life there together? What then?

Ben went into the luxurious bathroom, turned on the shower with its half dozen shower heads, and stood there as cold water stung him, sobered him after an hour of anger and hope and fear that had threatened to unman him. He had to be clearheaded. He had more calls to make, plans to make, a life to begin.

But what then? his mind continued to nudge at him. What would he do if Eden was determined to keep him from his son? What would he do? What *could* he do that would not end up destroying them all?

Six

Eden scrubbed her face, splashing cold water on her eyes as she did her best to repair the ravages of nearly a full night of weeping. Grieving.

She had lost Ben. Not that she'd ever had him. Not that she'd know what to do with him if he still wanted her. Which he couldn't. Not because she hadn't told him about Sawyer five years ago. But because she hadn't told him in the two days he'd been back in her life.

But that wasn't the worst. She had gotten over Ben once, or so she knew she had to tell herself, convince herself. She could get over him again.

What she could not get over, could not banish from her heart, mind, or future, was the fact that Sawyer's father had a right to meet him. Be with him. Have a hand in raising him.

It was impossible!

Sawyer's home was here, in Texas. With his cousins and aunts and uncles. His grandmother. With his mother.

She'd already heard some of Ben's feelings about

family, opinions he'd delivered to her quite casually, but opinions Eden was sure Ben believed in from the bottom of his heart.

His son. His heir. The next Sheikh of Kharmistan. To Ben, Sawyer's future must be cast in stone, pre-ordained, predestined. A straight path that led from Texas to Kharmistan, and ended there.

But Sawyer's life was here. Her life was here, her family, her career, her future. Kharmistan might be a nice place to visit, to hear Ben talk about his modern, liberal country, but she wouldn't want to live there.

She wouldn't want Sawyer to live there. She would not *allow* Sawyer to live there!

The part of the night Eden hadn't spent pacing and crying, she'd spent on the Internet, looking up everything she could about Kharmistan; its history, geography, customs. Its rulers.

There was no question Kharmistan was a beautiful country. The sweep of desert, the beauty of oases, the absolute splendor of seaport cities. Universities. Theaters. A landscape that offered beauty in every direction.

All it needed was a little less sand, a lack of oil and gas, and the addition of a world-famous casino, and Kharmistan had all the fairy-tale charm of Monaco.

Eden had reread her woefully insufficient notes

on Ben, her notes on Yusuf Nadim. She'd read them with new eyes, new insight, finding words between the lines that told her that Ben might say his country was peaceful, but the presence of the ambitious Nadim took a lot of the milk and honey out of Ben's assertions.

The man was ambitious. Cassius was ambitious. Brutus was ambitious.

And her son, by damn, was not going to be entered into any equation that had anything to do with Yusuf Nadim's ambition.

"You're going to get frostbite if you don't stop trying to drown yourself with cold water," Mary Ellen Fortune said, leaning her shoulder against the doorjamb as she looked into the bathroom. "It's eight o'clock, Eden, and Sawyer is downstairs, having his breakfast. I thought you were going to talk to him before the sheikh arrives."

Eden grabbed a hand towel and pressed it against her face, appalled to learn that she still had more tears to cry, and that they were threatening to fall once more, for her mother to see.

She put down the towel and turned to look at her mother. "How is he this morning? Is he excited about Holden's idea of taking he and Hercules out for a ride, checking fences?"

"Do you mean, was I surprised to see him up and

dressed at six o'clock, looking out the front window for his Uncle Holden?''

Eden managed a weak smile as she walked past her mother, back into the bedroom that had been hers as a child, that was still decorated in pinks and whites, with her collection of dolphin figurines lining the windowsill.

''How did you keep him out of here, Mom? It sounds like Sawyer thinks this is like Christmas morning. This year he was bouncing on my bed at four in the morning, begging to go downstairs and see what Santa had brought him.''

Mary Ellen sat on the edge of the four-poster bed, shrugged her shoulders. ''You know Sawyer, Eden. He's always had this sixth sense about you, zeroing in on your moods in a way I wish your father might have tried to zero in on mine, God rest his soul. He even warned me not to wake you, as 'Mommy had a bad night, Grandma, and we shouldn't bother her.'''

Mary Ellen shook her head, shrugged once more. ''From the moment he was born, Eden, I told you there was something very *different* about that boy. There are times I think he can look straight into my soul. Lucinda says the same thing. She told me once that she believes Sawyer has the soul of either a shaman or a great chief. Odd, isn't it?''

''Sawyer is his father's son,'' Eden admitted,

stepping into faded jeans, pulling on a red and white plaid shirt she'd owned since college. She wasn't going to try to impress Ben this morning, be at all attractive to him. "I just didn't know it, that's all. Didn't know that my sturdy little man was a prince. God," she said, collapsing onto the side of the bed, beside her mother. "Guess that answers the question about heredity versus environment, doesn't it?"

"Not really, darling," her mother said, patting her shoulder. "I've always considered you to be our own special princess. And I haven't yet met the Fortune who isn't at least moderately arrogant."

Eden put her arms around her mother, kissed her cheek. "What would I do without you, Mom?" she asked, then got to her feet, took a deep breath, and looked toward the door to the hall. "I guess this is it, isn't it? Time that I sat Sawyer down and told him about Ben, about his father?"

"I don't see how you can put it off, Eden. Not if you don't want somebody else to do the telling for you. Although I would advise putting on some shoes before you go downstairs."

Eden looked down at her sock-covered feet, then laughed. The laugh was a little hollow, definitely self-mocking, but it proved to her that life does go on, no matter what. That, even when the worst was happening, life still had to be lived.

* * *

"Hi, buddy," Eden said as she stepped out onto the front porch, to see Sawyer swinging around one of the posts as he kept an eye out for his Uncle Holden. "I don't think he's coming until about nine-thirty, you know."

"I know, Mom," Sawyer said, grinning at her. "I was just closing my eyes and trying to tell Hercules that I'd be seeing him soon. Aunt Lucinda says animals and people can communicate, if they love and respect each other. Hercules loves me, I'm sure of it. I'll bet he's up at the stables now, whinnying and pawing and waiting for Joey to come saddle him. Especially since I promised him a carrot."

"A carrot, huh? And would that be Hercules or Joey who gets it?" Eden asked, ruffling the thick black hair on her son's head before leaning down to accept his kiss on her cheek.

He took the hand she offered, and the two of them walked down the wooden steps to the front yard, beginning a walk that took them around the back of the house, and to the huge wooden jungle gym and swing set that had entertained Mary Ellen Fortune's children before there was ever any thought of grand-children.

Were there jungle gyms in Kharmistan?

"Are you happier this morning, Mom?" Sawyer asked as they each sat on their favorite swing, push-ing their toes into the soft dirt, setting the swings into a slow, soothing motion. "You didn't look real happy last night, when you grabbed me away from Uncle Holden and brought me back here. I am sorry I went outside without asking Grandma, but I thought you should know that it was time to say good-night to me. You always say good-night to me."

Eden smiled at him as best she could. Typical male! It was amazing. The child was five, and yet he could turn his own transgression into her fault without a blink of an eye. "And I've accepted your apology, Sawyer. All five of them, as a matter of fact. But you must understand how worried I was when Grandma called up at the main house and told us you were missing."

Who would watch over his nights at the palace? Would he always be surrounded by guards like Haskim? Would they wear swords, carry weapons under their robes? Would those weapons ever be necessary?

Sawyer ground the tip of his boot into the dirt. "It was dumb, and I shouldn't have done it. I don't need you to tuck me in. I don't even need a night-light anymore. Not much, anyway."

Were there night-lights in the palace?

Eden blinked back tears, averting her head as she felt Sawyer withdrawing from her. Not her baby anymore. Not totally dependent on her, at least not in his own mind. Were all five-year-old's like this? Or only Sheikh Barakah Karif Ramir's son?

Sawyer had been almost exclusively surrounded by adults since his birth. He'd become verbal quite early, mimicking his elders both in speech and manner. Mary Ellen swore he had the vocabulary of a child twice his age.

Besides being much too grown up, too solemn.

That was why Eden had enrolled Sawyer in play school when he was only three, to expose him to other children his age. And it had worked. Well, it had worked a little. According to Mrs. Apple, at the last parent-teacher's conference, Sawyer was still the acknowledged leader of every group, the child all the others looked up to, followed.

"A natural born leader, Ms. Fortune," Mrs. Apple had said. "After twenty-five years of this, I can pretty much tell what their grown-up pecking order will be, just from watching the children interact with each other. Sawyer is and will be a leader, not a follower. He's polite, well-mannered, much more mature than other boys his age. If only we could find a way to make him...well, shall we say a little less *autocratic?*"

Heredity and environment. That hadn't been a purely joking remark Eden had made to her mother. But, she still wondered, was her very mature little boy ready for Kharmistan? Was Kharmistan ready for him?

"Sawyer?" she began, taking hold of the chain of his swing, gently pulling the swing to a stop so that she could look at him. So that he could see that she wanted to talk to him. Talk to him seriously. "I have something important to tell you."

He hung his head. "I know, Mom. Put toothpaste on the toothbrush, right? I was going to, honest. But then I thought I heard Uncle Holden, and I—"

"Not that, Sawyer," Eden interrupted, her smile a little more watery than she wanted it to be. How she loved, adored this child! "Although we will discuss the matter of toothpaste later."

"Yes, ma'am," Sawyer said, rolling his eyes and grimacing comically. "We always do."

Eden took a deep breath and attempted to begin again. "Do you remember Uncle Logan's wedding, Sawyer? Do you remember asking me why Amanda Sue could have a daddy and you couldn't?"

"That was mean," Sawyer said, nodding. "I made you cry, didn't I, Mom? Uncle Logan said I made you cry. But if Amanda Sue could find her dad, and she's only a baby, why can't I find mine?"

Childish logic. It must all appear so simple to Sawyer, and yet so difficult. He wanted his daddy, and he should be able to find his daddy. Or his daddy should be able to find him.

"Sawyer…honey…life is…*complicated* some-times," Eden began yet again, then winced as she realized she was talking to her son as if he were at least twelve, or perhaps twenty. "Let's walk," she said, taking his hand, setting off in the direction of the open range, bright blue wildflowers waving in the breeze ahead of them.

"You do have a daddy, Sawyer," she said at last, stopping in the deep, fragrant grass, kneeling in front of her son, her hands on his shoulders. "I—I just didn't know where he was, so that I could tell him that he's your daddy."

"Where did you look? Maybe you didn't look in the right places."

Eden felt the blood draining out of her face. She hadn't looked anywhere. She had considered herself deserted, and taken charge of her life, done what had to be done, and refused to look back, refused to think about Ben Ramsey except very late at night, when she stood in the hallway and looked in at her sleeping son, wondering where his father slept that night.

But she couldn't tell Sawyer that. She simply couldn't.

The boy couldn't understand the anger she'd felt, the heartbreak, the betrayal. And she would not al-low her son to despise his father, which is what he would do if she told him how Ben had left her, almost without a word. How Ben had not bothered to come looking for her after she left Paris, had not come to America, to Harvard, where she was back at her classes, studying and coping with morning sickness.

"Mom? Are you all right? You look funny. Sort of like that guy last night, the one with the funny name. His face got all funny, too. And all we did was talk."

This was her opportunity, and she had to take it before it slipped through her fingers. "Sawyer, that man last night. He...he's your father. I didn't find him, and he didn't find us. We just sort of stumbled into each other, three days ago, in San Antonio. But he's so very, very happy to have seen you, to know that he has a son."

"He didn't know about me?" Sawyer's posture was ramrod straight as he stiffened under Eden's hands. "*You* know, Mom. Why didn't you tell him? Because you didn't know where he was? Why didn't you tell me? You knew where I was, Mommy. I was here, with you. We could have gone and looked for him together."

Damn Ben Ramsey! Damn Sheikh Barakah Karif Ramir! Damn him for lying to her about himself, even as he took her into his arms, into his bed, told her he loved her, wanted to spend his life with her.

Damn his lies, his duplicity, his supposed chivalry, his arrogance and pride that kept him from following after her when he thought she'd told him to stay away. Would a man truly in love simply obey the scribbled brush-off of a note left with some hotel concierge?

She wasn't the only guilty party here, dammit! It wasn't as if she'd gone to ground, hidden herself away. And it wasn't as if she would have had any success locating Ben Ramsey, even if she had gone looking for him.

So why was Sawyer looking at her so accusingly? And why was she feeling so guilty?

"Your daddy might be able to answer some of your questions better than I can, Sawyer," Eden said at last, watching as her son bit his lip, as one heartbreakingly large tear escaped the absurdly thick fringe of long dark lashes around his too bright eyes, rolled down one unnaturally pale cheek.

"I won't talk to him!" the boy said at last, his voice high, almost shrill. "I won't see him, and I won't talk to him. I hate him! And I hate *you*, too!"

Eden sank back onto her heels, both hands pressed to her mouth, watching as Sawyer ran back toward her mother's house, toward Holden who stood on the back porch, his arms held open, to gather his sobbing nephew close against his strong chest.

"Talk to him, Holden, please," she whispered as

her brother lifted Sawyer high onto his shoulders, went back into the house. "Talk to him, make him understand what I can't understand, what's impossible to explain. Explain to Sawyer. To Ben. And then let me find a way to make Ben understand that his son doesn't really hate him."

Eden sat on the old rocker, where she had been ever since watching her mother and Mrs. Betts drive off toward the main house, Mary Ellen saying she felt her daughter and Ben would feel more free to talk if no one else was in the house.

She could smell the honey buns her mother had baked before she left, and even summoned a small smile as she realized her mother still believed there was nothing so bad that it couldn't be helped by a little home cooking and a talk around the kitchen table.

She could picture it now. "Hi, Ben, you hate me, your son hates you, I bungled the explanation so that he hates me, too. Perhaps you'd care for some butter on that bun?"

Eden watched the road, waited for the small cloud of dust that would tell her Ben's limousine was on the grounds, heading toward her mother's house. She watched, and she waited, and she wished she could think of something even moderately coherent to say when Ben arrived. Anything to say. Anything at all.

And then he was there. The black limousine appeared along the curving road to her mother's house, situated two miles away from the main ranch house, an eternity away from the safety of her mother, her family.

Haskim hopped out of the front passenger seat the moment the limousine came to a halt, running to the rear compartment, throwing open the door.

Ben Ramsey did not get out of the car.

Sheikh Barakah Karif Ramir—His Royal Majesty, Big Chief Emir, Prince Whatever—of the ancient land of Kharmistan, however, was there in all his glory.

Thanks to her stint on the Internet, Eden knew Ben was wearing a princely *aba,* an ankle-length coat of many colors, this one striped unevenly in dark purple, blue, and orange, all displayed on a pure white background. His *kaffiyeh* was of whitest white silk, banded by an *agal* of spun gold around three thick coils that held the cloth on his head.

As he mounted the steps to her, the *aba* moved with him, revealing a peacock-green silk lining, as well as the dark purple caftan beneath the robe and worn over a pure white *kamis*—the name, she knew now, for what was really only a long white shirt.

Only Ben's shoes were Western. Or as Western

as Gucci could be. The rest of him, from his *aba* to the imperious look on his tanned, handsome face, the steely glint in his dark eyes, was pure Kharmistan.

This, his look seemed to say to her, *is who I am. This,* the set of his jaw told her, *is who my son is. When we speak, we will speak with these truths before us.*

"Your Highness," Eden said shortly, rising, opening the screen door and motioning for him to precede her into the house, toward the smell of honey buns, toward the reality of this comfortable home Eden had to hold on to as hers, as Sawyer's.

Ben inclined his head slightly, allowing her to understand that, yes, he was her superior, then swept through the doorway, his robes whispering as he went, taking the desert into her mother's house, taking centuries of Kharmistan pride and arrogance and sovereignty and employing it to take possession of her mother's house.

He was, Eden decided, looking for a spitting contest, and believed he was the obvious winner. Well, he hadn't counted on the Fortunes of Texas. They'd been winning spitting contests for a lot of years, and she, as a Fortune, wasn't about to roll over and play dead just because the blood of desert princes ran in his veins.

Now, if she could only convince herself of the

truth of her own bravado, somehow put some of the starch back in her knees.

"Your mother's house, I understand," Ben said, motioning her to a chair, as if he acknowledged where he was and still set himself up in the role of host. "My son visits here often?"

"Oft—often. Yes, often." Oh, this was going well. Why didn't she just bow down and kiss his Guccis? "Sawyer and I are lucky to be surrounded by a loving, caring family," she went on, raising her chin a fraction. "A very protective, powerful family."

"I am sure this is so, Eden," Ben answered, picking a photograph of Sawyer up off an end table, taken the day the boy had first sat on his pony, Hercules. "My son rides?"

Eden felt herself begin to melt, because even the Sheikh of Kharmistan could not keep the pain out of his voice as he asked his question. As he knew, yet again, how very much of his only son's life he had missed, could never be a part of through anything more than photographs.

"He...um, Sawyer was sitting a pony almost before he could walk," she told him, crossing to the fireplace and taking down another photograph, this one of their son at the age of two, sitting on Santa's lap at a San Antonio department store. "Would you like to have them?'' she asked, handing him the second photograph.

"Yes, thank you. I would like to have these. I would like to see every photograph and video you have of our son. Where is he? Have you told him about me?''

She motioned toward the kitchen at the back of the house. "Would you like some coffee, Ben, a piece of cake? My mother baked some buns this morning.''

"You did not tell him.'' Ben's dark eyes skewered her. She wouldn't have been surprised if he called for Haskim to drag her away to the dungeons.

"I told him,'' she answered when she could find her tongue. What was going on here? She felt as if she'd been caught up in some Hollywood version of *The Sheikh and the Texas Girl,* or something just as inane. "Ben, for crying out loud—''

"And what did he say? How did he react?''

There was only one safe way to take a fence, and that was head-on. "He says he hates you and doesn't want to see you. But that's all right, because he hates me, too. You didn't gain a son last night, Ben, I— I lost one. So you can stop acting the big bad sheikh now, all right, because you're not impressing me— and then help me figure out what in hell we're going to do now.''

She sat on the nearest chair and dropped her head

into her hands. She fought tears as she took in deep breaths, willing herself back under some semblance of control. A control that broke entirely when Ben knelt in front of her and took her into his arms, pulling her against his shoulder.

"Oh, God, Ben," she said on a sob, "what am I going to do now? He's my baby. My own sweet baby. How can I make him understand what happened? How can we ever make this right, for all of us?"

He held her as she cried, as all the fear and the heartache, combined with the hazy knowledge dawning at the edges of her brain that Ben was holding her close for the first time in more than five long, lonely years, washed over her, robbed her of any strength, both physical and mental.

He smelled so good. His muscles were so strong, so solid beneath her grasping fingers. Memories forcibly buried so long ago returned in a hot rush of physical awareness, her traitorous body remembering how he had held her, how he had loved her.

"I believe in fate, Eden," she heard him say, whispering the words into her ear as his warm lips brushed against her bare skin.

"I believe in luck, Ben. Bad luck," Eden replied, pushing herself out of his arms, struggling to gain her feet, to put some much needed space between them. "It can't be fate that separated us, but bad luck. And our own pride. Now Sawyer's paying the price.''

Ben rose to his full height, his robes still impressing her even as she wished she weren't so easily intimidated by the trappings of his royal office.

''Our son does not hate you, Eden. You must give him time to accustom himself to the idea that he no longer dreams of a father, but that I am here. That I intend to stay, to learn to know my son as he learns to know his father. Deeper explanations will wait until he is older, more able to deal with complete truths. For now, I will move slowly, at Sawyer's pace. We will become friends.''

Eden rubbed at her damp cheeks with the back of her hand. ''Oh, really, Ben? And how long do you intend to stay here in Texas? A few weeks? A month? Because you don't know your son. He's not going to fall into your arms if you show up with a couple of toys and some stupid, romantic explanation it would take six gallons of water to swallow. Not your son. Not my son. You don't know him.''

''I know you, Eden, and I know myself. The fig does not fall that far from the tree.''

Eden didn't know how, but his last statement reached her, touched her, even brought a small smile to her lips. ''That's *apple,* Ben. The apple doesn't fall that far from the tree.''

He shrugged, stepped toward her once more.

"Are the two so different, Eden? Are we all not more alike than we are different?"

She put out her hands, hoping to hold him at arm's length. Because he was too close to her. His proximity frightened her. Her reaction to his proximity terrified her. She had been shocked at his reappearance in her life, shocked to learn who he was, what he was.

That shock had kept her from thinking too much about how she had once loved him, how she might still love him. Love could only cloud her reason, end with her making decisions based on her own need, and not on what was best, safest, for Sawyer.

"We can't do this, Ben," she warned him, warned herself. "We can't muddy the waters with some sort of transitory involvement that has no chance of being more than that. I know you've been hinting at starting up where we left off, and I'm flattered, Ben, truly I am. But I'm also Sawyer's mother. Any decisions I make will be to benefit him. They won't be to scratch an itch we both had almost six years ago."

Ben tipped his head to one side, looked at her closely. "'Scratch an itch,' Eden? Is that what you thought we were doing in Paris? I do not believe you."

That was understandable. Eden didn't believe herself. But this was important. She had to divide Ben and herself from any decisions made about Sawyer and Ben.

"I don't believe it really matters whether you believe me or not, Ben," she said, running a hand down the back of her head, along the single braid. "What matters is that you're not going to use our son to get me to topple back into bed with you."

He looked at her for a long time. Watched her closely, silently, assessingly. "Very well," he said at last, turning away from her. "If you would be good enough to contact me at my hotel when you have come to your senses, I will be awaiting your call. Until then, Eden, I will busy myself making my own very legal, very proper arrangements as concern visitation with my son."

"You—you wouldn't do that, Ben," Eden said, rushing after him as he walked toward the door. "You wouldn't put this whole mess into the hands of lawyers, would you? You wouldn't force the issue, make Sawyer do something before he has had time to…to…to *accept* that you are his father? And it'll hit the papers, Ben, you can count on it. Somebody in the lawyers' office will sell the story to the tabloids. God! You can't do this, Ben!"

The eyes he turned on her were cold and hard, empty of anything except an almost palpable distaste directed toward her. "You would deny me my son, Eden, even as you say that you are not doing so.

You would deny yourself, turn away from even the chance we might build on what was begun in Paris. I am not so willing to deny myself, Eden. I will see my son. One way or the other, I will talk to him.''

"Oh, all right, all right!" Eden took hold of his arm, pulled him back toward the center of the room. "I'll admit it. I can't do this without you. Sawyer deserves to meet you, you deserve to meet him. Only we have to separate the two of us from our feelings for Sawyer. You can see that, can't you?''

"You might see that, Eden," he answered quietly, picking up the photographs of Sawyer, looking at them again. "I do not. We are a family, no matter how much you may deny that fact to yourself." He looked up, looked deeply into her eyes. "I do believe in fate.''

Eden returned his look, somehow not flinching at either his expression or his words. "If you could summon Haskim, Ben, I will show him where to put your bags,'' she said at last, knowing that the only thing worse than having Ben here, talking to Sawyer, would be to not have him here, talking to Sawyer.

Ben gave her the ghost of a smile, not a smile of victory, but one that promised a truce if she would allow it, then went outside to speak to his servant.

Moments later, Haskim was walking into the room, a large suitcase in one hand, a three-foot high stuffed white plush Arabian stallion with velvet bridle and jeweled saddle tucked under his other arm. Eden had no idea where Ben had found the toy, but she doubted she would ever become accustomed to the man's resourcefulness.

"Ben, that won't work," she warned him, pointing to the toy.

"What, this?" he said, and now his smile was wide, the sweetly innocent smile that had won her heart so many years ago. "This is not for Sawyer."

"Oh, no, Miss Eden Fortune," Haskim said, putting down the suitcase and bringing the toy over to her, handing it to her. "This is a present from His Highness meant for you. The young prince, his present is still in the trunk of the limousine."

The servant grinned. "A video game, Miss Eden Fortune. One I should be honored to demonstrate for the prince, as my children have the same game at home, in Kharmistan. I have reached Level Three, although my little Melek, who is only four, she has climbed as high as Level Five."

"Thank you, Haskim," Ben said, his voice kind, not impatient at all with his servant's explanation. "I believe you may now take the bags upstairs?"

"Oh, yes, yes," Eden said, still holding the plush animal, even stroking its wide-eyed muzzle. "Upstairs, Haskim, second door on the left. Ben?" she then asked as Haskim bowed, retrieved the luggage, and made his way toward the staircase.

"You do not like it?" he asked. "Another woman I would give diamonds. But you are not other women, Eden. If I am to find your heart, I would be careful to direct my feet down the correct path."

She looked at him, shook her head. "As I've said once before, Ben—you're good. You're very, very good. Now, if you want to get out of that very impressive costume and into some jeans, maybe you and I can finally ride out and find Sawyer?"

Seven

Ben was comfortable in the saddle, but not in his skin. Not when he knew the next minutes would be the most important of his life.

He could see Holden and Sawyer in the distance. Holden at ease in the saddle of a roan gelding, Sawyer riding a black-and-white pony more suited to his age and size. Even from this distance, Ben could see that his son had the relaxed, natural seat of an instinctive rider, his hands held high, his knees close to the pony's flanks, his heels well back.

One day he would ride through the streets of Kharmistan beside his father, dressed in ceremonial robes, sitting upon the back of a fine Arabian stallion.

Ben could see him now. See how he would look once dressed in the trappings of a young prince. A *kibr* of vermilion silk, trimmed in golden braid, worn over a snow-white *tobe,* a similar snow-white *kaffiyeh* on his head, held in place by a black *agal.*

Even his mount would be colorfully outfitted, its

bridle dangling with colorful ribbons, his saddle gilded with gold.

Ben would ride, and Sawyer would ride beside him. Their people would line the streets as they rode by, cheering, throwing flowers at the young heir to the throne of Kharmistan.

And Eden would be riding with them, all gold and white in her *khurkeh,* looking every inch a queen.

Dreams. Ben had dreams. He saw them so clearly in his head, waking or sleeping. His people would love Sawyer. They would love Eden. Their lives in Kharmistan would be full, happy. Glorious.

Except that Sawyer looked very much at home here in Texas, in his jeans and plaid shirt, a too large cowboy hat worn low on his head.

How could Ben take his son away from the only home he had ever known, the only family he had ever known? The boy did not know Kharmistan even existed.

But Eden did.

And that, Ben felt sure, was the problem.

"Holden's telling Sawyer to join us," Eden said, pulling her mount to a halt. "And, from the set of my son's shoulders, I'd say he's thinking about disobeying him. Maybe I should ride on ahead, talk to him, and then bring him back here."

Ben nodded his agreement, still looking in the

direction of his son, who remained several hundred yards away, a world away.

And then it happened. In the midst of hope, the unthinkable. Holden's mount reared crazily, tossing his rider onto the ground. Sawyer's pony, obviously terrified, took off like a shot, cutting out across the open range.

"Rattlesnake!" Eden shouted, pulling a rifle from her saddle even as she dug her knees into her mount and set off in an instant gallop.

Ben's range-trained mount moved right along with hers. "Attend to your brother. I will get the boy," he shouted, then leaned low over his horse's neck, urging the animal to greater speed.

He had no rifle, but knew from Eden's quick reaction that her experience would be Holden's salvation. Cutting off to his left, he rode toward Sawyer's horse at an angle, covering more ground to meet up with the boy rather than to chase him.

His horse was faster by far than the pony, but the pony was near-crazed with fear, its ears flat against its head, its stubby legs flying across the ground as Sawyer held on for dear life.

And the pony was smaller, which did not make Sawyer's rescue easier. Taking hold of the pony's reins could bring the animal down, and Sawyer with him. All Ben wanted to do was to get his son *off* the horse and into his arms.

The chase took less than a heartbeat, more than a year...

Ben was close now, could see Sawyer's face, see the fear there, yes, but also the exhilaration of riding across the open range at a full gallop. Ben felt sure this was his son's first experience at a gallop, as he could not imagine Eden allowing him such freedom at his young age.

But the boy was holding on, if too tightly, and he was holding his own. Ben's heart swelled with pride, clenched with fear.

There was the echoing crack of rifle fire in the air, and the panicked pony nearly lost its footing, its eyes rolling widely.

"Kick your legs free of the stirrups and get ready to let go of the reins," Ben called as his angled ride put him side by side with the smaller pony.

"No!" Sawyer yelled at him. "I can stop him."

"He has the bit between his teeth, child," Ben told him even as he pushed his own mount closer, brushing against the pony slightly, trying to turn it, slow it from its mad, headlong dash.

The fine Texas-bred horse beneath him was brilliant, beginning to herd the pony as it would a calf cut off from the main herd.

"Lean forward, Sawyer. Keep your hands bunched on the reins, but loosely, so that he relaxes his bite. Allow him to think he has control, and then show him that control is yours.''

Slowly, with Ben ready to grab Sawyer off the pony if he believed it necessary, the pony began to tire, began to yield to the larger horse, to the man riding him. Ben vowed to line his clever American mount's stall with the finest oats and hay if, together, they could pull this off.

''I did it!'' Sawyer exclaimed at last as the pony tired, eventually slowed to a walk. All while Ben's heart remained lodged in his throat, all while his chest felt very near to bursting with fatherly pride in this brave child's performance.

''That you did, son,'' he told him as he bent and at last took hold of the reins. Lightly, just to help Sawyer decide where to next turn his mount. ''Now we will return to your uncle and allow your mother to yell at me.''

''She'll yell at you? Why?''

''We will allow her to explain, I believe. Ah, do you see? Your uncle is on his feet, and appears unhurt. And I can see the fire in your mother's eyes from here.''

''Are you afraid of her?'' Sawyer asked, looking up at his father.

''I respect her as your mother, Sawyer,'' Ben explained as they continued to ride back in Eden's direction. ''As do you. Therefore, we will listen to her closely, and agree with everything she says. Then, this afternoon, we will take your pony out again, and we will teach him some manners.''

Sawyer's smile was wide, and quickly hidden behind a childish scowl. ''You're not my father, are you? Mom says you are, but I don't believe it. My father wouldn't have stayed away from me so long. He's dead, and you're not anybody I want to know.'' He looked down at the ground, then up at Ben once more. ''I think.''

''For now, Sawyer, I would ask only that you allow me to be your friend.''

Sawyer looked toward his mother, then back up at Ben. ''You're a good rider,'' he said, his expression still wary but his shoulders not quite so squared.

Ben smiled, content with his son's compliment. ''You are a good rider, Jamil Altair Omar, with a brave heart and a determination that reminds me of a young prince who must have been a sore trial to his parents.''

''Ja—Ja*meel?* Who's that? My name is Sawyer.''

''Your American name is Sawyer,'' Ben told him as he looked toward Eden yet again, saw the mingled relief and worry on her face. ''But you are, as of this moment, also Jamil Altair Omar. Jamil, which means handsome, as long as you remember that handsome is as handsome does. Altair means flying eagle, as a salute to both your free spirit and your birth nation's fine symbol of greatness. Lastly, you are Omar, meaning my first son, something our people must know and respect.''

As Sawyer frowned, Ben shook his head, adding, ''But we will leave all of this for later.''

''Ja-meel,'' Sawyer repeated, as if trying out the name on his tongue. ''I like that. It almost sounds like I'm a Ninja Turtle, doesn't it? There's this pile of old videos at the ranch, and I've seen the Ninja Turtles. Mom—did you see me?'' he called as they reached the spot where Eden and Holden waited. ''Did you, did you? I stopped Hercules all by my-self.'' He looked sideways at Ben. ''Well, almost by myself.''

Ben watched Eden closely, sensing that she felt torn between wanting to take Sawyer into her arms and cover him with kisses—and wanting to shake him for being so happy when he had just frightened her nearly to death.

''He was never in any danger once I reached him, Eden,'' he said, willingly sacrificing himself to spare Sawyer, and to give Eden the release of tension she most definitely needed.

She did not disappoint him.

''After you *reached* him he was very definitely still in danger,'' she stormed, glaring at him. ''You could have grabbed him off Hercules at any time, but you didn't. What was that, Ben? Some sort of

Arabian rite of passage—learn how to do it or die a glorious death in the attempt? How *could* you just watch? My God, Ben—he's only a baby!''

Holden lifted Sawyer down from the saddle and took him over to inspect the dead rattlesnake…and out of earshot as Ben dismounted, walked up to Eden.

''We have a stubborn son, Eden,'' he told her quietly. ''And a very brave one. But do not think that I would put our son in danger, not while there is a breath left in my body. Now, go to our child, hug him as a mother does. But do not fuss, do not call him your baby when he wants to be a man. Allow him to glory in his fine accomplishment. Lessons will come later, when he is receptive to them. And one thing more, Eden. We will not argue about the child in front of him. He needs to feel love, and security, not fear.''

Eden stared at him levelly for a long time. Looked him up and down, measuring him…finding him wanting. ''I don't believe you. You think you can disappear for years, then show up and immediately start telling me how to raise my son? You arrogant bastard. Sawyer is my son, Ben, *mine*. And you can go to hell,'' she said at last, before turning on her heels and going to her child.

''Eden is a good mother, Ben,'' Holden said as the two men sat on the front porch of Mary Ellen

Fortune's house, sipping lemonade his mother had brought to them. "A damn good mother. And, yes, a little overprotective. It isn't easy, you know, being both father and mother to a child. Going it alone. Knowing that, when you get down to it, you're all that child has. That he's all you have, that he's your whole world."

"Her son's world has grown larger," Ben said, knowing he was being unreasonable, but unable to stop himself. "Her son's world has grown to include a father, a people, another heritage."

He looked at Holden. "He is a little boy, yes, but he is also Prince Jamil Altair Omar Ramir, heir to the throne of Kharmistan. Eden does not want to believe this, refuses to believe this."

Holden rolled his eyes. "Can you blame her?" he asked, spreading his hands as he repeated, "'Prince'? That's a big chunk to swallow, Ben, for any of us. Especially that mouthful of names you just rattled off. You do move fast, don't you?"

Ben drained his glass, set it on the table beside him. "She believes I will take him from her," he said, sighing. "She will not believe that I want her, have wanted her—loved her—for years. And why should she, Holden? I left her, I did not come back. I could be promising your sister anything, just so that I can get Sawyer on my jet and relocated in my own country.''

Holden scratched at the back of his neck, wincing a little as he said, ''We've all read the papers, seen the stories on television. Hell, Ben, there was even a movie about fathers spiriting their children overseas and not allowing their mothers to see them, to take them home. You're a powerful man, Ben. You could probably get away with kidnapping Sawyer, and there wouldn't be a damn thing Eden could do about it. Although you'd have to know we'd fight you with every last dollar of Fortune money.''

''I am the bogeyman now? The thief who comes in the night, stealing babies?'' Ben smiled sadly as Holden opened his mouth to speak. ''No, my new friend, do not apologize. Such things have happened, and we both know that. But Eden also knows me, she knows my hopes for my family. I told her of my hopes that first day, before I knew Sawyer existed. It is me that she is rejecting, not Sawyer's father.''

Holden was silent for a long time, the two men sitting on the rocking chairs, letting the silence of a vast land envelop them.

At last Holden spoke again. ''You know, Ben, I don't think Eden's had a date in six months. Hell, I don't think she's had more than a half dozen dates since Sawyer was born. Certainly no one you could call a boyfriend. She works—works hard—and she takes care of Sawyer. That's been Eden's life since you last saw her.''

"I blame myself for that," Ben said, staring into the middle distance. "I remember the joy in her eyes when we were together in Paris. I have not seen that same joy these past days. Only fear."

"Right," Holden said, getting the bit between his teeth, just as Hercules had done an hour earlier. "So maybe you ought to try to do something about that. Maybe you should take it slower with Sawyer, take it one day at a time. No more of this Prince Jamil stuff, for starters. And spend your time concentrating on Eden, concentrating on reminding her how much she loved you, how much you loved her. I mean, hell, Ben, you're a nice guy. Really. But you sure can come on strong. Moving in here, making demands…''

"I am an arrogant man," Ben said, turning to smile at Holden. "Eden said that. She is probably right. I am more accustomed to giving orders, having them obeyed without question. But, unfortunately, there is more involved here than courting Eden, as you have suggested. There is the matter of Sawyer, and the presence of my chief advisor, who must not learn of Sawyer's existence until Eden and I have come to an agreement."

Holden immediately went on full alert. "Sawyer could be in some sort of danger?"

Ben shook his head. "No, I do not believe so. Not physically. But I have always believed it is best to begin as you plan to go on. That means I want the announcement to my people of Sawyer's existence to come from me, not from Nadim. You Americans have a saying in your football, as well as in times of war—the best defense is a good offense. I cannot allow Nadim to take the initiative with my people. That could make Eden's acceptance, Sawyer's acceptance, more difficult. Do you understand?"

"You've really got your hands full, don't you?" Holden asked. "And here I am, giving simplistic answers. Take Eden out on a few dates, romance her, find what you left in Paris. I promise, Ben, from now on, no more Dear Abby advice. I'll keep my big mouth shut."

"No, my friend," Ben said sincerely. "I value your advice, as much as I appreciate your love and concern for Eden and Sawyer." Then he smiled. "Besides, I think you are correct. I love Sawyer, flesh of my flesh. That love was instant, the moment I learned of his existence. But I loved his mother first, Holden. I still love her. And, instead of fighting her, I should be letting her know how much I love her."

"And Sawyer? We had a small talk, before you and my sister and the rattler showed up. Even though he's confused, perhaps somewhat angry and afraid, he's pretty damn excited about having a daddy. But if he's taking his cues from Eden, and he probably is, he won't let you see how thrilled he is unless he believes his mother is as happy, too. Eden may be very protective of Sawyer, but that protectiveness cuts both ways."

Ben stood, as did Holden, and the two men shook hands. "I will be returning to San Antonio later this afternoon," Ben said, having come to a decision. "I will speak with Sawyer before I go, and then to Eden. I will ask her to come with me, so that we might work out a solution that is best for Sawyer, for all three of us. And I will stop making demands," he ended, smiling.

"And we'll keep a close guard on Sawyer for you, keep him here on the ranch where this fellow Nadim can't find him," Holden promised. "You're going to work this out, Ben, I'm sure of it. Just give my sister her head for a little while longer, the way Sawyer did with Hercules, and she'll come around."

"Well, if that isn't lovely, Holden," Mary Ellen said, stepping out onto the porch. "Comparing your own sister to a headstrong horse?"

Holden winced and apologized to his mother, kissing her cheek, and taking his exit with more haste than ease, waving at Ben and saying, ''You're on your own, friend—I'm outta here!''

Ben gestured for Mary Ellen to sit on the rocker Holden had just vacated, then sat himself.

Eden's mother was a beautiful woman, a woman with the sort of classic features that would continue to be beautiful far into her eighties. Her skin was porcelain fair, her eyes a clear blue, her thick, wavy red hair making a striking frame for her face.

Eden, it would seem, had taken the best of both her mother and father, had combined that with a beauty of her own. Ben knew he could look at the mother and see the daughter as she would be in thirty years. A woman of refinement. A woman of intelligence. Of great courage. A woman a man could respect, admire. And love.

''So, Holden's been giving you pointers on the gentle art of correctly romancing a woman?'' Mary Ellen said at last, her blue eyes looking very much amused. ''If I were to tell that to Lucinda, she'd laugh long and hard.''

''Theirs was not an easy courtship?'' Ben sat back, relaxed into the rocker. He had a friend in Mary Ellen Fortune, he could sense that, even if he was not sure he had an ally.

''I wouldn't be giving away any family secrets if I were to tell you that my husband made it a condition of his will that Holden find and marry a 'respectable' woman before he could inherit. No, theirs was not an easy courtship. But they've found love now, and their marriage is all I could have hoped.''

''And what do you hope for Eden, Mrs. Fortune?''

''You're a nice man, Ben,'' Mary Ellen said, obviously measuring her words carefully. ''But you have no idea what Eden went through, coming back here, believing herself deceived, deserted. And then, of course, there was her disgust with herself for having acted so irrationally, having been so careless as to have become pregnant.''

Ben lowered his head. ''We were both careless, Mrs. Fortune. I do not believe a woman to be solely responsible in such matters.''

''No, of course you don't. And that's all well and good. But it docsn't change the fact that Eden believed she had behaved as impulsively, as irresponsibly, as her father had been known to do. Don't get me wrong, Eden loved her father, very much. But she didn't respect him, and had vowed to herself that she would never be like him. Never hurt other people through her own rash actions, sacrificing common sense for the thrill of the moment.''

She took a small white handkerchief from her pocket, dabbed at her eyes. ''But then she stood herself up, shook herself off, and got on with it. Came home to have her baby, completed law school, and then took Sawyer and herself off to her first job in California. She wanted to stand on her own two feet, you understand, prove to us—and to herself—that she could be independent, that she could be a good mother and father to Sawyer.''

"I—I did not know any of this," Ben said, wishing yet again that he could go back, that they both could go back, do things differently. "She must have hated me, and with good reason."

"She never hated you, Ben," Mary Ellen said firmly. "Quite the opposite, as a matter of fact. I suppose she inherited that from me—loving one man, and one man only, no matter what."

She smiled then, a sad, sympathetic smile. "Which doesn't mean she'll admit as much, even to herself. You've got a long row to hoe, Ben, a long row to hoe. But that's not why I came out here. I wanted to tell you that Eden is upstairs, packing. She insists on leaving Sawyer here and returning to San Antonio this afternoon. I believe she thinks it's the only way she can get rid of you. So, while you're sorting that out in your head, I thought you could go have a talk with Sawyer. He's in the family room, quite happily watching some Ninja Turtles videos."

Eden stood at the archway leading into the family room, keeping herself out of sight as she watched Ben and Sawyer. She'd been standing there for more than five minutes, and she still was having difficulty believing that Ben was lying on his stomach, doing some very wicked dragon slaying with the help of the joystick to Sawyer's favorite video game.

She didn't know why she was surprised, since the Ben she had known in Paris had delighted in simple pleasures, wasn't at all the starchy, formal Sheikh Barakah Karif Ramir she had met again a few days ago in San Antonio.

Was it Ben who had changed? Or was it her? Did he treat her differently now because of their long separation? Because she was Sawyer's mother? Or because now Ben was a head of state, a powerful sheikh, a man more used to command than to obedience? Because he was now more accustomed to the stiff formalities of royalty than to the easygoing ways they'd enjoyed in Paris?

Who was this man? Was he still Ben Ramsey? Or had the Ben she'd known, loved, been replaced by an intimidating, almost frightening prince? Had he been transformed from the loving, laughing companion she'd remembered, into a man who would take her son from her, without so much as a thought to how that would kill her?

Eden looked at her son, her baby, her whole life, her reason for living. Sawyer was sitting cross-legged beside Ben on the carpet in front of the television, cheering his father on as another dragon bit the dust. Looking at them in profile, seeing the same dark hair, the same dark eyes, the same shape of their heads, Eden had to fold her arms tightly across her stomach to not moan and give herself away, alert them to her presence.

Was there nothing of her in Sawyer? Were Ben's genes so strong that they had overruled hers on everything from the color of Sawyer's eyes to the way he bit the bottom corner of his lip as he concentrated…just as Ben was now biting on the bottom corner of his own lip. What had she been? A mother? Or incubator to a prince?

She looked at Ben, and saw her son in thirty years.

She looked at Sawyer, and saw the boy Ben had been.

And her empty arms ached. Her heart ached. Her very soul cried out in silent despair.

The game ended when Ben allowed his warrior to be vaporized so that their son won the game. That was nice of him, Eden knew, and smart, too. As her mother had always said, ''Allow a child to win at games until he's seven, to build his confidence and assure him he can win—but after that, take no prisoners! Children have to learn the sting of failure, too, in order to appreciate success.''

Eden was doubly grateful to Ben for deliberately losing to Sawyer, because he might have thrown a tantrum if he'd lost. Not that Sawyer threw a lot of tantrums, but the ones he threw were usually humdingers. She didn't want Ben to see Sawyer in anything but the best possible light.

"You're going now?" Sawyer asked as Ben got to his feet, looked toward the archway, his left eyebrow raised, silently telling Eden he'd known she'd been there all along. His dark eyes invited her to watch, to see how he and his son were getting along—how brilliantly they were getting along.

This was punishment, she was sure of it, even as she also believed Ben was about to prove to her how important a father could be in her son's life. How important Sawyer was to Ben's life as well as to hers.

"I am leaving now, yes, as I told you I must," he said as Sawyer clambered to his feet, pushed one faintly dirty hand through his unruly mop of dark hair. "But we will have that lesson with Hercules another time, I promise. We will see each other again soon."

Sawyer dipped his head. "And then you'll go away again," he said, his bereft tone sneaking into Eden's heart, cracking it. "Tommy Barnes isn't going to believe me when I tell him I have a dad. Not if you're not here. And he's got *two*. I should be able to have one, shouldn't I?"

Ben went down on his haunches, putting himself

at eye level with his son. He placed his hands on Sawyer's shoulders, looked deeply into his eyes. "You have a father, Jamil, and I am he. I am with you always, even when I cannot be here. My love shelters you, protects you, watches over you. Always believe that, Jamil, for I will never lie to you. You are blood of my blood, blood of our ancestors. In time, you will learn the fullness of that gift, of that obligation. For now, however," he said, ruffling Sawyer's hair, "we will content ourselves with speaking to each other every night on the telephone. Remember?"

Sawyer nodded, although his posture remained ramrod straight, almost brittle. "At seven-thirty, just before I go to bed. I remember."

"Good. And now, if you would not mind, I would ask a favor of you, Jamil."

"Of me? Sure. What is it?"

"I would ask if I, your father, might kiss your cheeks, hold your strong body against mine, just for a moment. If I promise not to go—how is it said?— all *sappy* on you, will you allow that?"

Sawyer bit his bottom lip, considering the request. "I suppose so," he said at last. "Go ahead."

Eden already had her hands pressed hard against her mouth to cover an involuntary sob. But she closed her eyes now, twin tears spilling over to run down her face, as Ben took her son's head between his hands, then slowly, reverently, kissed each soft, baby cheek.

Sawyer threw his arms around Ben, in the innocent acceptance of youth, and Eden watched as Ben pulled him close in an embrace, kneeling before her son. Their son. Loving him. Giving love.

She turned on her heels and ran back through the house, the screen door slamming as she stumbled outside onto the porch.

"Eden? What's wrong?"

Eden wiped at her wet cheeks, then turned to see her mother sitting in her favorite rocker.

"Nothing, Mom," she said, her bottom lip trembling. "Everything."

"I see," Mary Ellen said, shaking her head to prove that she didn't "see" at all.

"He called him Jamil," Eden blurted, leaning against one of the heavy wooden porch posts for a moment, then pushing herself upright once more, beginning to pace. "His name isn't Jamil, dammit! It's Sawyer! How dare he do this? Who in hell does he think he is?"

"I believe, darling, that he thinks he's Sawyer's father," Mary Ellen said calmly. "As you got to pick his American name, I suppose Ben felt he was entitled to choose his Arab name. Jamil? That's rather nice, isn't it?"

"Oh, good, Mom," Eden snapped angrily. "Side

with him. I'm sure he'll be grateful. Grateful enough to maybe let you come to the airport to see *Jamil* off as he whisks him away to Kharmistan. Or haven't you thought about that one?''

"Kharmistan *is* a part of Sawyer's heritage, Eden,'' her mother pointed out gently. "And it would perhaps be better if he arrived there with a name more suited to his role as heir to the throne. But you can't seriously tell me you believe Ben would whisk Sawyer off—kidnap him?''

Eden stopped pacing, stared at her mother. "No, I don't believe he'd sneak him away in the middle of the night, or anything like that. But it isn't as if we could arrange some civilized visitation rights such as weekend visits, now is it? He'll probably want him every summer, when school's out. And how do I compete with a kingdom, Mom? It won't take long before Sawyer wants to visit more often, until he wants to live there. I mean—a kingdom? A palace? His every wish and want catered to, day and night? It would be like Disney World for Sawyer. I'll lose him.''

"You'll lose him? Eden Fortune, I'm ashamed of you!'' Mary Ellen said, getting to her feet. "Are you even *listening* to yourself? You're Sawyer's mother. He *loves* you. If you don't have faith in yourself, Eden, or trust in Ben, for goodness' sake have some small bit of faith and trust in my grandson!''

"Oh, Mom," Eden moaned, allowing herself to be gathered into Mary Ellen's loving embrace. "I'm so scared. What am I going to do?"

"You're going to follow your heart, darling," her mother told her quietly, stroking her hair. "In the end, that's all you can do. That's all any of us can do."

Eight

The sun was setting before the limousine carrying Eden and Ben approached the suburbs of San Antonio and the mellow brick house on Edgewood Drive. Theirs had been a mostly silent drive, punctuated only by the ringing of Ben's cell phone and his quick, clipped conversations in Arabic to whoever was on the other end of the line.

Eden's Arabic was less than nonexistent, but she did believe she had caught the name Jamil at least twice during one of the conversations.

So, she'd decided, that's how it was going to be, was it? Ben making plans, hiding those plans from her? What had he been saying? Worse, what had he been planning? She resolved to phone her Uncle Ryan out at the ranch later tonight, to impress on him yet again that Sawyer must never be alone, never be left unprotected.

Unprotected? From his own father? Did she trust Ben so little?

"Ah, we are here already?" Ben commented, bringing Eden back to the moment. "I had not realized. Eden, have I left it too late to tell you that I have planned a small surprise for this evening.''

She immediately went on the alert—her jangled nerves tangling themselves around her heart. ''A small surprise?'' she asked warily. ''What kind of small surprise?''

The limousine pulled up against the curb, and Eden looked out to see a white delivery van parked in the driveway. The words Custom Catering were painted on the side in rather elegant, dark blue script.

''What's that?'' she asked, pointing toward the van, hating the fact that her hand was trembling.

''If we can trust Haskim's powers of translation,'' Ben told her, smiling rather sheepishly, ''I imagine it is a four-course dinner for two. You do still enjoy French cuisine, Eden? I ordered—had Haskim order—the same menu we enjoyed together in Paris the first night we met. Do you remember that night, Eden?''

Her mouth had gone dry, so that she was forced to swallow down hard before she could answer. ''I remember, Ben,'' she said at last, as the driver came back to open her door. Haskim, who obviously had been the ear on the other end of Ben's cell phone calls, and who had followed them in another car that had magically appeared at the ranch, seemed to have been given the night off. "I also remember that neither of us ate more than a few bites."

"We were too busy talking, weren't we?" Ben agreed as he nodded a farewell to the driver and slipped his arm around Eden's waist, escorting her up the walk, to her front door. "Will tonight be very different, do you think?"

"That—that depends on what you want to talk about, I suppose," Eden replied as she dug in her purse for her keys, wondering how it was that her legs were supporting her, how her feet knew to move along the walkway.

Because there was a strange lightness in her head, a curious buzzing in her ears…and a definite flutter in her stomach.

Her entire body had gone all strange on her. With what was left of her mind Eden decided that what her traitorous body was doing, was about to do, was to betray her completely, falling once more under the spell of Ben Ramsey, her Paris lover.

"Ben…" she said, looking back toward the smiling men carrying large chafing dishes up the walkway…then looking at Ben, her eyes begging him to help her. "I can't do this. Please understand. I just can't do this."

Ben took her key ring from her unresisting fingers, opened the front door. "The kitchen is down this hallway, gentlemen, and to your left. You know where to set up your table?''

"Yessir," one of the men said, shifting the bubble gum in his mouth. "In front of the fireplace, that's what our orders say. And then we're to make ourselves scarce until tomorrow morning, right? Bubba—I mean, Francois—was mighty put out that he wouldn't be serving you. Had himself all done up in his tux and everything."

"My most profound apologies to Francois," Ben said as the three workers passed by them, heading into the house. Then he winked at Eden, who had inexplicably gone from abject fear to near hysterical laughter, finding she had to lean against the doorjamb or otherwise collapse in a puddle of laughter.

"Bubba Francois," she got out at last, wiping at her streaming eyes. "Supposedly the finest caterer in the city. Maybe we ought to rethink this, Ben. I mean, I don't know about you, but I'd have loved to hear his French accent."

Her sense of humor, that had just betrayed her as badly as her nervous system had done a moment earlier, evaporated as Ben took hold of her elbow and steered her inside, toward the stairs.

"Not that you are not always lovely, even in jeans and T-shirt, but I believe we have at least a half hour before our dinner is served, if you wish to go

upstairs and change into something more suited to
our candlelight dinner.''

Overbearing, arrogant, bossy man! How dare he
tell her to take herself off upstairs and change into
something more ''comfortable.'' Who—*what*—did
he think she was?

''Your Highness?''

Eden, who had been ready to tell Ben to go to
hell, and what he could do when he got there,
whirled about to see Haskim standing just outside
the still-open door. He was holding a garment bag
and small overnight suitcase.

''I don't believe this! Do you actually think
you're going to be staying *here?* God, Ben, where
do you come off—believing I'd invite you to stay
here?''

Haskim stepped past her, heading for the staircase. ''I have your suit, Your Highness, and all else
that you shall need for a formal dinner. Miss Fortune? Perhaps you might direct me to the proper
room upstairs, so that His Highness can refresh himself, dress for dinner?''

Eden looked at the grinning servant, then to an
almost contrite-looking Ben, who reminded her of a
dangerous wolf draped in a sheepskin trying to
blend in with the rest of the flock.

''Oh, go ahead, Haskim,'' she said at last, glaring
at Ben to let him know that, whatever he had

planned, it wasn't going to work. "Upstairs and to your right. The room with the blue-and-white-striped wallpaper."

"Thank you, Eden," Ben said as Haskim climbed the stairs. "This is difficult for both of us, I know. Our conversations about Sawyer are best not conducted in public, but I felt that we might be more comfortable if we at least had the trappings of civilization surrounding us as we converse."

She looked him up and down. Sniffed. "Yeah, Ben. Right. I believe that—as much as I'd believe that Garth Brooks has always had a hankering to sing opera."

"Who?" Ben looked at her questioningly, clearly not understanding the comparison.

Which, yet again, served to send Eden into nervous laughter. "You honestly don't know, do you? Hasn't old Garth hit Kharmistan yet? He's hit the rest of the world. The next time you see Sawyer, you might want to ask him to sing *Friends in Low Places* for you. But be warned—don't tell him his father never heard of Garth Brooks. I mean, the child might never recover."

She stood beside the staircase, holding on to the newel post until Haskim reentered the foyer, then she bounded up the stairs, singing loudly, "'I've got friends in *low places*...'"

It wasn't until she had stripped out of her clothing

and was standing under the shower in the bathroom attached to the master bedroom that the unnatural hilarity that had seemed to be her defense against hysteria at last deserted her completely.

She put her arms out in front of her, pressing her hands against the tile wall on either side of the water-control knob, and bowed her head, letting the pulsating water from the shower head beat down on her neck, her upper back.

The water massage didn't help. Turning on the waterproof shower radio and tuning it to a country station, praying the music would drown out her own thoughts didn't help. She was still wound as tightly as a drum, her senses heightened, her heart refusing to maintain a steady beat for more than a few moments at a time.

Then she heard Willie Nelson singing about a good-hearted woman in love with a good-timing man. Eden had always considered that tune to be her mother's theme song, and her father's greatest failing.

Was she doing it again? Was she once more going to think like her mother…and act like her father? The last time she'd thrown conscience and responsibility and possible consequences to the winds she'd had her heart broken.

And she'd gained Sawyer, the child who'd healed that broken heart.

Eden turned off the radio, grabbed a bottle of shampoo from the shelf inside the large shower stall, and began washing her hair with an intensity that brought fresh tears to her eyes.

She knew what he wanted.

He wanted her to remember.

God help her, she did remember. She would never, could never, forget...

She'd been wandering through a small Paris museum devoted to less well-known artists when she'd stumbled over a threshold and straight into Ben Ramsey's helpful arms.

She had raised her head, her mouth already forming the words "Thank you," when her eyes met those of her rescuer and she forgot what she had been about to say.

Those eyes. Those dark, laughing, seen-everything, done-most-of-it eyes.

And then, as her tongue did everything but twist itself into a knot, he smiled, and with that smile she knew that her life had suddenly, unexpectedly, changed forever.

When she at last could speak, when he answered, the words were unimportant. They both somehow knew what the other had meant:

"I—I—" she stammered.

"And I," he'd said feelingly, his voice deep as a

velvet midnight even as he threaded her arm through his and guided her toward the exit.

She went with him, unprotestingly, feeling safe and yet in perilous danger at the same time.

There had been a small restaurant only a few hundred feet from the museum door, and within minutes Eden was seated across a table from this magnificent physical specimen straight out of any girl's dreams.

He'd ordered for them both in flawless French, then tasted the wine before nodding that, yes, *mademoiselle* could now be served. The waiters, all five of them, had all but fallen over themselves with happiness that *monsieur* had approved the wine, but then discreetly melted into the dimness at the merest lift of her companion's hand.

It was magical. More than magical.

She was Cinderella at the ball.

She was Sleeping Beauty awakened by only the promise of a kiss.

She was Eden Fortune, hopelessly out of her depth, and ready to throw more than twenty years of calm common sense straight out the window without a moment's regret.

"Speech, at this moment," he'd said to her at last, "would almost seem redundant, would it not? For I know you, have known you since the beginning of time. You do feel that? I pray you feel as I do."

From another man, at another time, in another

universe outside this small world they seemed to have created between themselves, Eden would have laughed lightly and said something like, "Well, that's a come-on line I haven't heard before."

But they were in this time, they were together, the two of them, in this small world. And he was not another man. He was like no man she'd ever met.

"I am Ben," he said when she didn't speak. "Ben Ramsey. And you—you are beautiful."

At last she did answer, smiling at him, smiling with her eyes, her lips, her heart. "Now *that* one was more than a little hokey, Ben," she told him, waving her hand at his outrageous compliment.

"*Ho*-key?" His smooth brow furrowed questioningly for a moment, and then he sat back in his chair, grinned with the openness of a child. "Yes, it was, was it not? My apologies—"

"Eden," she told him, knowing he was waiting for her to fill in the blank. "Eden Fortune. Now, if you'd please explain what we're doing here, how we got here, *why* I allowed you to bring me here— well, I'd really appreciate it. Because, and I'm not ashamed to say it, I've never done anything this impulsive in my entire life."

He smiled once again, that smile calming her, relaxing her, even as she felt the same physical thrill she'd experienced earlier. "Do you believe in fate,

Eden Fortune?'' he asked, taking her hand in his across the small table, lifting it to his lips. ''I do.''

Before the evening was over, an evening spent talking, and laughing, and doing their best to ignore the hand-wringing waiters who took away course after course of nearly uneaten delicacies, Eden also believed in fate....

''But I don't believe in fate anymore. And I sure don't believe in history repeating itself!'' she assured herself firmly as she dried her hair in front of the bathroom mirror, then scraped the thick dark brown mane back into a French twist.

She all but stomped to her walk-in closet, clad only in small wisps of black silk, and reached far into the back of the closet to pull out a plastic wardrobe bag. She couldn't believe what she was about to do, but she was going to do it anyway.

Just to prove that she was now immune, her heart hardened, her resolve intact...and her silly dreams forever banished into the fairyland that had been that first night in Paris with Ben.

They met on the stairs, Eden coming from the master bedroom, Ben walking down the hallway from the opposite direction. She knew where he'd been, could see it in his face.

''The room you changed in is at *my* end of the hallway, not the direction you just came from,'' she told him, noticing the far-off look in his eyes. "The house isn't that big, Ben, you couldn't have gotten lost."

"I visited Sawyer's room," he said honestly. It was not an admission of any sort of guilt, not a statement even slightly tinged with apology. It was simply a statement of fact. He had been in his son's bedroom.

"I see," she said as she preceded him down the stairs. "And did you find anything that interested you? See any lack that you and your bottomless pockets will have some underling fill before Sawyer comes home? I didn't think you'd stoop to buying your own son, Ben, but I guess a lot has changed in nearly six years."

"Time has not changed how beautiful you look in that dress, Eden," he whispered into her ear as they both stopped at the bottom of the stairs to watch the small procession of caterers trailing through the foyer on their way out the front door.

"All done, sir," the last caterer said, holding out a piece of paper that was obviously the bill for the company's services.

"Haskim was supposed to take care of this. Perhaps this company does not accept the Kharmistan National Bank's credit cards?" Ben quipped facetiously as the caterer looked at Eden, clearly puzzled.

"You still don't carry money with you, Ben?" Eden asked, shaking her head. "Do you know how…how *arrogant* that is of you? I'll go get my purse."

"There is no need," he told her as he reached into the inside pocket of the absolutely fantastic dark blue suit he was wearing—she had refused to look at him while they were in the upstairs hall, for fear her knees would melt. He'd been wearing a dark blue suit the first time they'd met. A dark blue suit, a whiter-than-white dress shirt against his tanned skin. He'd remembered. She remembered.

He extracted a gold money clip thick with folded bills, and began peeling them off into the caterer's hand. As each new bill was dispersed, the young caterer's eyes grew wider, soon to be followed by a toothy grin that nearly split his face. "Thank you! *Thank* you, sir!" he said at last, then turned and nearly ran out of the house, probably sure Ben would soon discover his mistake and ask that half the bills be returned to him.

"You understand the exchange rate between Kharmistan money and the American dollar, right, Ben?" Eden asked as she brushed past him, heading for the kitchen and a tall glass of cold water. "No, don't bother to answer that. Of course you do. You just always tip one hundred and fifty percent of the bill. That guy probably won't stop running until he hits the doors of the nearest mall.''

"You are angry with me, Eden, not the caterer. I needed a service performed, at very short notice. Those men provided that service. It is as simple as that.''

"And as complicated,'' Eden told him, taking a glass from an overhead cabinet and then filling it with ice water from the dispenser compartment on the front of the refrigerator. "How high do your servants jump when you say their names, Ben? Have you any idea how unusual it is to have your sort of absolute power in today's world? Have you any idea how having this same sort of power could warp Sawyer's view of real life?''

"Sawyer is a child, Eden,'' Ben said, his tone maddeningly reasonable when she was begging, itching for an argument, some way to get him out of her house, out of her life. "He will have a personal servant, yes, but he will also have a small allowance that is not in the least extraordinary. He will also have his duties, his lessons. At Sawyer's age, Eden, I was already speaking French with my language tutor. Does Sawyer have these opportunities here?''

Eden ground her teeth together, then glared at Ben. "He can count to one hundred and fifty and knows his name, address, and telephone number.

And the names of all the Power Rangers," she tacked on, feeling like a terrible mother, experiencing all the defensiveness and insecurities of the single mother trying to raise her son alone.

Raising a *prince,* a future king, alone absolutely defeated her.

Then she rallied, lifted her chin defiantly. "He's five years old, Ben. Life expectancies being what they are, what they will be, he'll probably live to be ninety or more. There's more than enough time for him to learn what he needs to know. Right now he needs to learn how to be a child."

"Yes, Eden, Sawyer is a child. A child with two parents who love him. But you would deny him half of his family, half of his heritage. Not because you do not love him, not because you do not love me, but because you are frightened. I understand."

"You *understand?* Well, bully for you, Ben." The half-empty glass hit the far wall, shattered to the floor, leaving a wet stain on the wallpaper. Eden stared at the growing stain, unable to comprehend that she had been the one who'd thrown the glass. Unwilling to believe she, who prided herself on her control, had lost that control so swiftly, so violently.

Yet she was also surprised she'd had enough control to not throw the glass at Sheikh Barakah Karif Ramir's head.

"Oh, my God," she whispered, burying her face

in her hands. "This isn't happening. None of this can be happening. When will I wake up? Nobody can survive in a nightmare like this."

Ben stepped forward, slid his arms around her shoulders, allowed her to cry into the fabric of his suit. He held her gently, mumbling nonsense words into her ear, soothing her as he would a frightened animal.

And she let him. She had to, for she was too exhausted to fight him any longer. She let his strength surround her, breathed in the intoxicating cologne she remembered from Paris, gave in to a moment of pure trust in a man who held the ability to destroy her happiness forever.

When he led her into the family room, sat beside her on the couch, she kept her head buried against his shoulder, slowly admitting to herself that she took comfort in his presence, that this man who had come back into her life, turning that life into a complete shambles, was also the only person to whom she'd ever want to turn to for help.

"I love him, Ben," she said at last, sitting back and rubbing at the tears on her cheeks. "I love that child *so much*. I want what's best for him, even if what's best for him destroys me. But you have to give me time, Ben. I'm not ready to lose him to you, to Kharmistan, to his future as the next sheikh. My

God, Ben, Sawyer can't be a prince—he still sucks his thumb at night!''

Ben reached out, patted Eden's damp cheeks with the soft linen handkerchief he'd pulled from his pocket. ''Eden, have I asked you to give up your son?''

She sighed, caught her breath on a dry sob. ''No, Ben. No, you haven't. You're even willing, so you say, to make us a family, take that family back to Kharmistan with you. Which we both know is impossible, don't we? Your people will accept Sawyer—he's you as a child all over again—but I doubt they'll accept his mother. Remember, Ben, to them I will be the woman who kept the heir to the throne hidden in America for five long years.''

''And the international tabloid press will have themselves a field day, won't they, Eden? The Hidden Prince… Sheikh Ramir Hoodwinked Into Marriage… Eden Fortune, Her True Story… Texas Seductress Bears Elvis's Love Child. Is this what you are thinking?''

Ben tipped up her chin with his index finger, smiled into her eyes. ''I can think of at least a dozen celebrities who would be very grateful to see the tabloid feeding frenzy turned away from them and onto us for the next year or more. Have you ever had your photograph taken by some idiot half falling out of a helicopter as you try to take a simple swim in the ocean, Eden?''

''That's not funny,'' Eden said, shivering at the thought of such a total lack of privacy. ''And I won't put Sawyer through it. I won't.''

''And I would? Eden, think. You did not know I was who I am. One reason for that is that my face has never appeared in any of those lurid tabloids. I do not allow it.''

''How—'' Eden shook her head. ''Never mind, I probably don't want to know how you've managed that, do I?''

''I doubt you would,'' he agreed, taking her hand and helping her to her feet. ''Now, let us forget all of our problems and enjoy our meal. All right?''

Eden looked at the small table for the first time, at the gleaming silver, the mass of thick candles and stubby roses that made up an informal centerpiece, the silver, standing bucket holding crushed ice, one bottle of chilled wine, one of spring water, and two upturned glasses. ''Only because I'm hungry,'' she grumbled mulishly, waiting as he pulled out her chair for her.

Ben pulled the chilled glasses out of the ice and poured her a measure of wine before he lifted the silver covers in front of them, revealing a clear, cold consommé. ''Our first course in Paris, as I recall,''

he said, sitting across from her. "*Bon appetit,*
Eden."

She picked up her spoon, as she had done so
many years ago, and sampled the consommé. It was
probably wonderful. It smelled wonderful. But now,
as then, she couldn't taste it. All she could do was
gaze across the table, see Ben's smiling face, his
laughing eyes. She felt the intensity of his look, the
absoluteness of his intentions.

And she felt all of her resolve, her resolutions,
slipping away from her. She had to do something
fast. Or else she'd be lost.

"You'd do anything to get Sawyer, wouldn't you,
Ben?" she asked at last…finally succeeding in eras-
ing his smile. "Seduction. Kidnapping, if seduction
didn't work."

"I love you, Eden," he said quietly, his voice
hard rather than seductive. "I came here for you,
remember. I did not know our son existed."

"And if I said I didn't believe you? If I said that
the damn near richest man in the world knew full
well where I was every minute since you deserted
me in Paris? If I said you always knew of Sawyer's
existence, but you just didn't give a damn? If I said
that it wasn't until your wife died that you decided
that maybe the American's bastard son was good
enough to show to your people, to make them happy
to see that your line would continue? If I said you

came here to get Sawyer, even if you had to romance the mother to reach the son? What would you answer if I said any of that?''

Ben slowly, carefully, laid down his soup spoon. ''You have already said it all, Eden,'' he pointed out quietly, a small tic having begun to work in his left cheek. ''I hurt you badly when I left Paris, and I am sorry for that. But until this moment I did not realize that I had destroyed you. I have persisted, doggedly holding to my memories, excusing you at every turn. But now I see the truth. You are not the Eden I remember. That Eden did not look at people and see ulterior motives, purposeful deceit. That Eden had an openness, a love of life that captivated me in an instant. I am sorry she is gone.''

Eden watched as Ben carefully folded his napkin, laid it on the tabletop, stood up. He was leaving. Dear God, he was leaving!

''No! Ben, wait!'' she said, hopping to her feet so quickly she nearly overturned the table. She ran to him, took hold of his arm with both hands. ''I'm sorry...I shouldn't have said any of that. I—I don't know what's wrong with me, Ben. I'm just scared. My whole world turned upside down when I saw you again. I'm *so* scared...''

And then she was in his arms. She didn't know how, she didn't know when, but one moment she had been tugging at his sleeve, begging his forgiveness…and the next they were holding each other, kissing each other, damn near devouring each other.

She felt her curls tumble free of their pins as Ben jammed his fingers into her hair, his hand at the back of her skull, pressing her hard against his mouth.

He wasn't being gentle. She didn't want him gentle.

Her mouth opened under the assault of his tongue and she breathed in the essence of him, fought with a thrust and parry of her own. She couldn't get enough of him, couldn't hold him close enough.

Almost six years. Six years since he'd touched her. Since she'd held him. Since they'd loved.

Too long…too long…too long apart.

Somehow, they were both on their knees on the beige Berber carpet, still holding each other, their mouths still fused. Eden felt her fingers ripping at Ben's silk tie, impatiently tugging at the buttons of his dress shirt. There was a lot to be said for those loose flowing robes she'd seen him in, imagined him out of without ever admitting as much to herself.

Cool air caressed her back as the zipper on her dress whispered open. The heat of a thousand furnaces scalded her as Ben's hands slid along either side of her spine, found their way beneath the wisp of her black silk panties, cupped her buttocks as he ground himself against her.

She finally tore her mouth free of his, taking in

great gulps of air before attacking his throat, his ear, the dark, curling hair on his now bared chest.

He bit her earlobe, nipped at her shoulder as her dress, so carefully preserved all these years, seemed to shred under his searching hands. They were two lonely, frightened people feeding off the strength of the other; searching, searching, for some sort of solace, some sort of temporary peace.

He kissed her breasts through the sheer black silk, suckled at her, drove her insane with his flicking tongue until he'd found the front closing of her bra and dispensed with one of the last, ridiculous barriers she'd built against him.

They were lying on the floor now. Eden on her back, her dark brown hair fanned out above her head. Ben above her, ruthlessly stripping off suit jacket and shirt, flinging them away from him.

Eden watched him through slitted eyes as he twisted from one side to the other, taking off his shoes and socks. She saw the beauty of his strong body as his muscles rippled with his exertion, and then went on the attack once more. She tugged at his zipper, pulled his slim hips free of his trousers, of the paisley silk boxers that were so unerringly in Ben's taste.

He straddled her even as he lifted her legs high, slid her panties down her legs, flung them away. She raised her arms, doing her best to take hold of him, to pull him down to her, to hold him and love him and never, never ever let him go again.

He came to her willingly, entered her in one swift movement, brought his body against her as he braced his arms on either side of her head, looked down into her face. "Is this wrong, Eden? Is this madness?"

She had no words for him, no answers, no explanations. Sensation gripped her, held her, urged her onward…to more, more…more…

So she answered him with her body, lifting herself to him, moving with him thrust for thrust as he resisted her grip on his arms meant to pull him down to her so that she could kiss him.

Instead, he kept looking at her, looking straight through her. His thrusts intensified, and that age-old rhythm reached a frenzy of blurred movement. Her climax took her and she opened herself to him entirely, without fear, without shame…without reservation.

Without a word of love from either of them…just this overwhelming physical need.

Or, Eden thought, maybe not.…

Eden woke in her own bed, with only a vague memory of how she had gotten there. She could remember feeling lighter than air, safe in strong arms.

She sighed, stretched, and immediately winced.

Her muscles hadn't been this sore since she'd dug that new flower bed beside the garage last summer.

And then she remembered why she was so sore...

"Ben?" She squeaked his name, even as she ran her hand over the mattress, feeling for his body.

All she discovered was empty space.

Eden pushed herself up into a sitting position, tugging the sheet around her as she realized she was naked. She pushed a riot of unbound curls out of her eyes, blinked in the morning light, and looked around the room.

Nothing.

No Ben. No male clothing. No nothing.

Just that same yawning empty space in her heart that had appeared in Paris the last time she'd awakened to find Ben gone....

Nine

"Come on, Mom, come on...answer the phone. For God's sake, answer the— Mom! Mom, hi, it's Eden. Is Sawyer there? May I speak with him?"

There was a small silence on the other end of the phone before Mary Ellen said, "I just looked at my bedside clock, Eden. You do know it's only six in the morning, don't you? Sawyer's in bed sleeping, just like you and I should be."

Eden paced, the cordless phone in one hand, her other hand raking through her tangled hair. Her heart was pounding like a trip-hammer, her mouth dry, her stomach tied in half a dozen knots. "Check on him, Mom. Would you do that? Please? I'll wait."

"Eden—"

"Mom, *please!*"

She heard her mother sigh, heard the sound of the receiver being placed on the night table. And then she waited. Waited forever...

"Eden?" Mary Ellen said, picking up the phone once more. "I'm happy to report that my grandson is sound asleep, his thumb firmly in his mouth and

Fred curled up beside him. Now, suppose you tell me what's going on?''

Eden couldn't suppress a whimper of relief as she collapsed into a kitchen chair and squeezed her eyes tightly shut. "I—I don't know…I just…I just…oh, Mom, I'm a mess!''

"Yes, I'd begun to sense that. Stay where you are, darling—you are at home, aren't you? I'll wake Mrs. Betts, put her in charge, and be on your doorstep in a little over an hour, all right? Oh, and Eden? For heaven's sake, sweetheart, stop looking for bogeymen.''

"…And then I woke up in my own bed. Alone in my own bed. Mom, he has to hate me.''

Mary Ellen sipped on her second cup of coffee as she sat across the breakfast table from her daughter. "Hate you? So that's why he made love to you, Eden? To *punish* you?''

Eden nodded, still slightly embarrassed after telling her mother what she'd done, what terrible, hurtful things she'd said to Ben last night. "I accused him of coming to America already knowing about Sawyer, planning to romance me until he could get his hands on his son. That's pretty despicable of me. The moment I said the words, I knew they were crazy, that the whole idea was crazy. Ben's an honest man, even if he did lie to me in Paris. But I guess I'm still having trouble getting over that lie.''

Mary Ellen lowered her cup to the tabletop, smiled wanly. ''Understandable, Eden. If he'd told you the truth about himself back then, you would have been able to go to him when you learned you were pregnant.''

Eden sighed, looked across the table at her mother. ''Boy, you're smart, Mom. When am I ever going to learn that you know everything? No, you're right, I wouldn't have gone to him. He'd left me, without more than a quick, vague farewell note. For all I knew, he didn't want anything more from me than a Paris fling. But if he knew I was pregnant with possibly the next heir to the throne of Kharmistan? I would have had the same fears then as I do now, wouldn't I have, Mom?''

''I imagine so, darling, and I don't think I would have blamed you. But now I've met Ben, and I like him, Holden likes him, your Uncle Ryan likes him. He looks straight into your eyes when he speaks, and never flinches. I believe him when he says he loves his son, that he would never do anything to hurt him. And I believe that he loves you, Eden, even though you must be driving him mad at the moment.''

Eden smiled sadly, self-deprecatingly. ''And to think I've always prided myself on being so sensible, so levelheaded. Boy, when I fall off the sensible wagon, I sure do it in a big way, don't I?''

''You've hurt him, Eden,'' Mary Ellen said gently, reaching out to take her daughter's hand in her own. ''There's no denying that. You two didn't make love last night. You punished each other, trying to prove that all that's left between you is physical passion, nothing more.''

Eden bit her bottom lip, sniffled. ''Ben must have proved that to himself, or he'd still be here,'' she said sadly. ''I've never felt so alone, Mom, as when I woke up this morning to see that he was gone. I didn't even feel that deserted in Paris, when I woke up to his note. I didn't fall out of love with Ben over the years, Mom—I think I'm more in love with him now than I've ever been. Waking to find him gone felt like someone had just cut off my right arm.''

''And Ben has to know that you really love him, Eden. He certainly would never have to fear that you're just some fortune hunter, out to make a match with a future king,'' Mary Ellen said, smiling, squeezing Eden's hand.

Eden smiled slowly, the smile growing wider. ''No, he wouldn't have to worry about that, would he?''

''That all said, darling—may I suggest you wear your favorite lovely butter-yellow sundress when you go to see Ben at his hotel this morning? Groveling is always easier to manage if you know you look your best.''

Eden's smile faded as she shook her head, sat back against the wooden kitchen chair. ''No, I can't go to him. Not this morning, at least. I've got to go into the office, check on a few things, even though I'm supposed to be on vacation. That will give me some time, give Ben some time. I'll call later, from the office, and ask if he'll see me at his hotel, maybe in time for dinner.''

''Still having cold feet, Eden?'' her mother asked as she gathered up their empty coffee cups, took them over to the counter.

''Yeah. Yeah, maybe I am,'' Eden admitted, going to her mother, wrapping her arms around her, pressing her head against Mary Ellen's shoulders as the older woman stood in front of the sink. ''But, mostly, I thought I should give Ben a little time to catch up on his sleep. It might have started off slowly, but ours was sort of a *long* night.''

''Eden Fortune!'' Mary Ellen said, turning in her daughter's embrace, her expression one of deliberate shock and nearly schoolgirlish delight. ''Shame on you!''

Ben fought with himself all morning. He'd gone to the phone a dozen times, planning to call Eden. To apologize. To grovel. To promise her anything if she'd only forgive him for loving her, for leaving her, for showing up once more to complicate her life.

When he wasn't warning himself not to call Eden, he was fighting the impulse to drive out to the Double Crown, to see their son. Not that he seriously believed Eden would spirit him away, hide him from his father.

There was so much love between Eden and himself, Ben was sure of that. Enough love for a lifetime, for two lifetimes.

Why was there so little trust?

Ben only relaxed after he'd called Mary Ellen Fortune's house and spoke to Sawyer himself, listening to his son's story about how he had spent the morning baking apple pies with someone he called "Miz Betts."

Not that he had truly believed Eden would hide their son from him…but it had been so good just to hear the boy's voice. He hadn't known it possible to love so quickly, so fiercely, not until the first moment he'd looked into Sawyer's eyes. Not since he'd first looked into Eden Fortune's eyes a lifetime ago in Paris.

Ben checked his watch for the thousandth time as he walked through the large entrance foyer of the Palace Lights Hotel, carrying an armful of packages as he headed for the hallway that would take him to the elevator serving the penthouse.

As sheikh, he shouldn't be worried about Haskim, who had to be worried about him, but he knew he should apologize to the servant. The poor fellow had to be having kittens, as Ben's English tutor used to say. Luckily, he knew Haskim's weakness for Godiva chocolates, and he'd bought the man a five-pound box of his favorites.

Because Ben had been walking for more than three hours, having left the penthouse suite without Haskim seeing him, without a single bodyguard to accompany him. He'd walked the streets of San Antonio, smiling at the people, striking up conversations with salesclerks. He'd bought a beer for another patron at a small bar he'd wandered into, and exchanged views on the weather, sports, and the international scene.

He'd discovered a music store and gone inside, picking up a CD Walkman and three Garth Brooks CDs, then continued his walk with the earphones on, listening to *Friends In Low Places,* and his personal new favorite, *Ain't Going Down Til the Sun Comes Up.* His son had very good taste in music. What an infectious, happy sound!

He found himself wondering if Eden might possibly teach him something called "line-dancing," and the Texas Two-Step, both dances having been partially demonstrated for him by the barmaid in that same cozy little bar.

Texans certainly did know how to have fun, right now, right in the moment. Bigger, wider, higher. Big land, big smiles, big hearts. He had fallen in love with Texas, that was for certain.

Ben hadn't felt this free, this unencumbered by affairs of state, the rigors of protocol, since he'd been with Eden in Paris. Now he was without Eden, in her home state. And yet walking the streets, seeing the sights, meeting the people had all combined to make him feel closer to Eden, to Sawyer, to the life to be enjoyed in Texas.

He would never take his son away from this free, open, easy life. Sawyer and Eden would always be a part of Texas, and Texas would always be a part of them. Only a fool wouldn't understand this.

Ben hefted the packages into his left arm as he turned a corner in the hallway that was open on one side, with several pathways leading into a four-story-high atrium garden. He was almost at the elevator when the sound of raised voices reached him and he stopped, listened, instantly alert to tones of anger coming from the midst of the near rain forest of tall plants, coming from a man, from a woman.

"I said I want my money *now*, you bitch! I got to get off the ranch and get out of town," Ben heard the man say.

"And I told you—you'll see it when I see it," the woman countered. "Dammit, you don't have a brain in your head, do you, Clint? How am I supposed to give you what I haven't got? I'm living on credit cards myself."

"Yeah, right. You're still living as high and rich as you always did. I never should have listened to you, Sophia. All your big plans, your schemes. 'We'll be rich, Clint,' that's what you said. Do I look rich? Do I look like I could last more than a couple of months on what you've paid me so far? I want that money. I *deserve* that money, especially since I don't seem to be getting the other part of what I wanted from this whole scheme. I'm tired of doing your dirty work for you! Maybe what you need is a dose of your own blackmail."

As Ben drew closer, concerned at the escalating rage in the man's voice, the threat of menace, the woman all but purred, "You've always been happy enough to take it out in trade before, Clint baby, haven't you? Now, why don't we just go upstairs to my rooms and—"

Ben's packages hit the floor at the sound of flesh hitting flesh, within a heartbeat of hearing the woman's yelp of shock and pain. Ben ran inside the atrium garden, and within another heartbeat his left hand was holding tight onto the collar of the man's shirt as he lifted him clear off the ground, put his face an inch away from the startled bully's now bulging eyes. "Only the lowest of curs would think to strike a woman," Ben growled at him.

"What the—" the man whom the woman had addressed as Clint stammered, then pulled back his right arm, obviously intending to smash his fist into Ben's jaw.

Well, Ben supposed that was what the man had intended. He decided not to find out if he was right or wrong. Instead, he dropped the man to the ground, pulled back his own right arm and delivered a short, sharp blow with the edge of his hand, aiming just below Clint's left ear.

The man went down with the abruptness of night falling on the desert.

Everything had happened so quickly. Ben had reacted, instinctively defended himself, before sparing so much as a glance for the woman now standing behind him, laughing in genuine amusement. He turned around, looked at her, frowned. What did she find so amusing?

"Oh, that was gorgeous! *You're* gorgeous, now that I've had a moment to check you out," the woman said, rubbing at her cheek, her rather avid gaze running over Ben, sizing him up, looking pleased with what she saw.

She was, he noticed, a beautiful woman, if he had liked his women fully perfumed and painted, which he did not. He also didn't like her cold, assessing blue eyes, or the way she deliberately smiled and pouted with her shiny pink-stained mouth.

She was beautiful, yes, but he instinctively knew she was something else. A predator.

The woman closed the space between them, taking hold of Ben's suit lapels with her long, pink-tipped nails, insinuated herself against him. "How will I ever repay you for saving me, my sweet knight in shining Armani?" she asked, her once hard, shrill voice now lowered to a sensual purr.

Ben gently but firmly removed her hands from his lapels, then said, "If you would like me to summon a policeman?"

The hard blue eyes blinked, reopened to show him a brief moment of very real panic. "No, darling, I think not," she then purred, recovering quickly. "But don't you have the most adorable accent, so nearly British, and quite wonderfully formal. I'll bet you have all the girls in your hometown just *drooling* over you, don't you?"

Clint began to groan as he lay sprawled on the brick pathway, and Ben turned, looked down on the man. "Perhaps you would wish for me to escort you through the lobby, so that the doorman can summon a taxicab. Your friend seemed rather angry, and you might not wish to be in the vicinity when he rouses."

"Clint?" The woman shook her head, her strawberry-blond curls bouncing, looking unnervingly childish when compared to the craftiness of those big blue eyes, the sarcastic set of those full, pouty lips. "He wouldn't dare hurt me. He's thickheaded, and dumb, but even Clint Lockhart isn't brick dumb enough to kill the golden goose. But you're right, Boy Scout. One of us ought to be hightailing out of here, and I think that'd be you. Don't worry, I can handle him."

Ben was more than happy to agree with the woman's suggestion, suddenly feeling what he wanted most at this moment was a long shower that would rid him of her touch, her cloying perfume. "I was happy to be of assistance, and am sorry I interfered, as you say you do not need my help," he said, giving her a very slight bow of his head, then walking back to pick up his packages he'd left in the hallway.

As he loaded the packages into his arms, he heard Clint groan once more, and then listened as the woman crooned to him. "Ah, poor Clint," she was saying. "Here, sweetheart, let me help you up, you poor thing. Oh, look at that bruise! How dare that nasty man take you by surprise like that? You would have blackened both his eyes, if he hadn't jumped you, wouldn't you? Well, Sophia will just have to kiss you all better. I can think of at least fifty places where I can kiss you all better, better than new. You want to come up to my suite now, don't you, sweetheart. Clint! Here? You can't want to take me here…where anybody could see us? Hmm…yes, that does feel good. That feels *so* good…*so* naughty…*so* exciting. No wonder I keep you…."

Ben shook his head and walked away, definitely planning on a shower. It would probably take him two bars of soap before he felt clean again.

Eden heard the receiver being picked up, followed shortly by a few clipped words in Arabic.

"Haskim? Is that you?"

"Miss Eden Fortune? Is that you? This is Haskim, yes."

"Yes, yes, Haskim. It's me. Would it be possible for me to speak with Ben—I mean, with His Highness?"

Eden heard Haskim speaking to someone in the background, then another voice came onto the line. A deeper voice, one tinged with disdain even as the words spoken were openly gracious. "Miss Fortune? I am Yusuf Nadim, Chief Advisor to His Highness. May I please be of assistance? This has to do with the business deal so recently closed with the help of your place of employment?"

Eden began to pace her small office, wondering if Nadim was giving her the brush-off on his own, or on Ben's orders. "Well, no, actually, sir, this is a personal matter. I—I really do need to speak with His Highness. Is he there?"

"We do not, as a rule, divulge such information to casual acquaintances, Miss Fortune," Nadim responded, all traces of cordiality fading under the weight of disdain. "You can, I am sure, understand the security reasons behind such a response."

"Oh, okay, you're right. Forgive me," Eden said, nodding, feeling foolish for nodding, for apologizing. "But is it possible to give him a message? Because I really, really do need to speak with him today. I can give you the number of my cell phone, as I'm leaving the office now."

"Your location does not concern me, Miss Fortune," Nadim told her shortly. "And I do not *take* messages. Haskim will assist you."

Eden pulled the phone away from her ear, stared at it for a moment, then placed it against her ear once more in time to hear that Haskim was back on the line.

"My most profound apologies, Miss Fortune, that this should have happened, but His Excellency asked that I give the phone over to him," Haskim said sincerely. "His Highness has gone missing today, deliberately stealing out of the hotel to be on his own, and His Excellency is not pleased. But I will give His Highness your message as soon as he returns. We, of course, are already aware of every phone number where you might be reached.''

"Gone—gone *missing?* Haskim, where did he go? Is he safe?''

"His Highness is most assuredly safe, Miss Eden Fortune. He knows where his possible enemy is, and he is not on the streets of your city. He has left with me the written message that, should you phone, he would be pleased if you were to meet him in the lobby of this hotel at six of the clock this evening, at which point he promises he will also allow me, his servant, to once again perform his duties of protector, for which I am grateful. Now, please, I must go. There are ears and eyes where I do not wish them.''

Eden was a mass of apprehension and tangled nerves by the time she arrived at the Palace Lights Hotel, stepping in out of the bright sunlight and removing her sunglasses, immediately searching the lobby for some sign of Ben, of Haskim.

Nothing.

She looked at her watch, swore under her breath when she saw she was ten minutes early. Ten minutes, a lifetime…they seemed equally lengthy at this point.

And then she saw him. Ben was entering the lobby from the smaller side lobby that led to the

atrium and the elevator to the penthouse suites. He
was walking swiftly, smiling, having already seen
her.

He didn't look like a man who was angry with
her, disappointed in her. He looked like a man in
love.

Eden felt her limbs turn into noodles, barely able
to support her.

It was all right. Everything was going to be all
right. It just had to be!

Haskim walked behind Ben, dressed in his exotic
robes, looking to his left, to his right, obviously taking his role of bodyguard very seriously. Eden was
now so relaxed she could even smile at Haskim's
severe countenance. The man obviously knew his
business, and his business was protecting Ben.

Even so, Haskim was taken unawares when a
man—Eden couldn't see his face—moved out from
behind one of the massive marble pillars and planted
himself right in front of Ben, blocking his way.

Haskim's hand went to his waist even as Eden
saw Ben gesture with one hand that the servant was
to stay where he was, that he could handle this large
man who looked angry enough to spit nails...or
snap Ben's neck.

Eden broke into as near to a run as she thought
she could get away with without slipping on the
floor tiles in her high heels, or bumping into several

groups of people who all seemed to have been disgorged at once from the large bank of elevators.

All her earlier nervousness evaporated, her worries over what she and Ben would say to each other, how they would act—to be immediately replaced by her intention of protecting Ben from attack. By the time she reached him, however, he and Haskim were speaking to each other in Arabic. Ben was speaking quietly, and Haskim was smiling broadly—and the threatening man was nowhere in sight.

"What—what happened?"

"And a good evening to you, Eden," Ben said, lifting her hand, placing a kiss against her nerveless fingers. The look in his dark eyes spoke volumes, the seductive movement of his thumb against her palm told her that he didn't hate her. Wasn't even close to hating her for what she'd said last night.

Why that made her angry, she'd never know. But how dare he stand there, acting as though he hadn't almost been involved in a fist fight.

"Never mind that," she said angrily, pulling her hand free. "Who was that crazy guy going after you as if he wanted to rearrange your face? What happened?"

Ben took Eden's arm and walked her through the lobby, toward the doors leading to the street. "What happened? Well, it seems I interrupted a lovers' quarrel earlier today in the atrium garden. I had been enjoying your city for a few hours, and was just returning to my rooms.''

Eden skipped to keep up with him, as he seemed in a hurry to be shed of the hotel. ''Lovers' quarrel? Interrupted? How?''

''By knocking that man into a bank of small shrubs, actually,'' Ben said as Haskim ran ahead, opened the door to the limousine that was waiting at the curb. ''I do not appreciate men who hit their women.''

Eden watched as Ben settled himself beside her in the limousine, as Haskim took up his place in the front seat, beside the driver.

Then she sat forward. ''Now, tell me how you got rid of him? I only saw his back, his clenched fists, but he looked ready to tear you into pieces.''

''I merely apologized for my error in involving myself in what I now believe to have been a highly private affair,'' Ben told her as the limousine slowed in front of a small, exclusive restaurant a few blocks from the hotel. ''That seemed to satisfy him, although I imagine Haskim's rather ferocious growl may have helped to make him feel amenable to accepting my apology. Ah, here we are. I do believe, Eden, that I owe you a dinner, since last night's was left...uneaten.''

Eden forced a smile, suddenly nervous once more, apprehensive once more.

She took refuge in silliness. "Oh, yes, last night's dinner. I have to tell you, Ben, you haven't lived until you've smelled escargot left out all night. I nearly broke the disposal, cleaning up everything before the caterers came to pick up their equipment this morning. But is that all you're going to say? That you owe me a dinner? Don't you want to talk about…about what happened between us last night?"

He cocked an eyebrow, looked at her with some concern. "Do you wish to speak of last night, Eden?"

She bent her head, wet her dry lips. "No, no I don't." She raised her head once more, looked at him as tears pricked at her eyes. "But we should, Ben. We should talk about it. Shouldn't we?"

He traced the line of her cheek with a single fingertip. "I believe we both understand what happened last night, Eden, and why. A postmortem seems unnecessary. What I wish to speak of this evening is what will happen in the future."

Eden nodded, greatly relieved that he didn't insist on a postmortem, that he understood how she felt, that she knew how he felt. "All right, I'll agree to that, if you agree to explain something to me. Why would Haskim believe you have enemies, when you told me you didn't? Are you safe here, Ben? Is Sawyer safe here? And why did I get the idea that your enemies, if you have them, traveled with you here to Texas, are in your penthouse with you? Nadim. It's Yusuf Nadim, your father-in-law. Am I right? Is he why you asked that I meet you in the lobby? He is, isn't he?''

"You ask questions like a lawyer, Eden. And I forgive you, because you are a lawyer. Now, come, Haskim is holding the door open for us. We will discuss all of this inside, over our meal.''

He made to move, to leave the limousine, but stopped as Eden placed a restraining hand on his forearm. "Is Sawyer safe, Ben? I have to know. Is my son safe?''

Ben placed his hand over her grasping fingers, squeezed them reassuringly. "Our son is safe, Eden. I would not have it any other way.''

She refused to let him go. "A very clever answer, Ben, but you're leaving something out, aren't you? And are you safe, Ben? Should I be asking that, as well?''

"We are not going to eat dinner again tonight, are we, Eden?'' Ben asked, his sigh more theatrical than chagrined. "Haskim,'' he said, speaking to his servant, "go inside, if you will, and recompense our hosts for the meal we will not be enjoying, then tell the driver to proceed to Miss Fortune's house.''

"Yes, Your Highness.''

"Did you see that, Eden?'' Ben asked as Haskim

bowed, then went to do his bidding. ''No questions asked, no explanations necessary. I give an order, make a suggestion, and someone is always eager to please me. I am accustomed to that. Absolute obedience. It has probably spoiled me these past years, since I assumed the throne. But you are taking care of that possible arrogance, are you not? Now I seem to explain, and to apologize, at every turn. Does this please you?''

Eden tipped her head to one side, slowly smiled. ''Yeah. Yeah, I think it does. So, Ben, do you like peanut butter and jelly sandwiches? They're Sawyer's favorite.''

Ten

"Creamy or chunky?" Eden asked, holding up two jars of peanut butter as Ben sat at one of the kitchen stools, enjoying himself as he watched her work.

"Which is our son's favorite?" he asked, as Eden had already told him that peanut butter and jelly sandwiches actually were her son's second most favorite food, running a close second to tacos.

"It's a toss-up, actually," Eden answered, retrieving the grape jelly from the door of the refrigerator. "But we'll go with creamy tonight, because I've got more of it, all right? And then, before your tongue sticks to the roof of your mouth and you can't talk, you're going to tell me what you did today. Starting with how you ran away from poor Haskim, and ending with why you felt we had to meet in the lobby."

"You are feeling comfortable with me again, are you not, Eden?" he asked, resting his chin in his hand as he watched her work, building two thick sandwiches for them. "That is probably because you now believe that I worship you with my whole heart, my entire body. And you are enjoying this feeling of superiority, I am sure.''

She bent her head over her task, but not before Ben could see the attractive flush of color invade her cheeks. ''If you mean, do I believe you love me, then, yes, Ben, I do believe it.'' Then she looked at him, saw his grin, and brandished the kitchen knife at him. ''God, you're arrogant! Even when you try to act the supplicant, or whatever it is you're doing.''

''And you love me?''

She sliced the two sandwiches, then carried the jelly jar back to the refrigerator, opening and closing the door with some force. ''Don't push me, Ben. Love is the answer—that's what the poets say. But that's not true. Love is the question. The first question, to be followed shortly by, 'Now what the devil do we do?'''

Ben knew what Eden meant. Yes, they loved each other. If they had come together last night in mutual need, they had also come together in love, even without either of them saying the words.

But was love enough? Could he ask her to give up her life here in Texas? Did she love him enough to do this? Did he love her enough not to ask her to do this?

''I will tell you about my day as we eat this delicious dinner,'' he declared, and her shoulders relaxed slightly, telling him that she was more than willing to drop such a volatile subject for something more mundane.

"You ran away from Haskim," she said, coming around the breakfast bar and sitting beside him. "That's a naughty, naughty sheikh. The poor guy was frantic when I spoke with him this afternoon."

"A panic for which I apologized," Ben told her as he reached for his glass of cold milk. "Haskim was, of course, appalled that his sheikh should so debase himself, and offered to leave my service if he displeased me so greatly. Do you see how it works, Eden? What seems reasonable in one culture, is not so in another. So," he said, grinning at her, "I gave him one of the Garth Brooks compact disks I had bought, and he is happy again, if still wondering if His Highness has perhaps slipped a gear or two since arriving in Texas."

Eden laughed, the sound happy, joyful. "Garth Brooks? Is that what you were doing, Ben? Shopping for Garth Brooks's CDs?"

He nodded. "And visiting with a very nice man named Bobby-Tom, and a barmaid who told me to call her Sugar. All in all, Eden, it was a very pleasant afternoon. After which," he added, knowing it was time, "I had a rather more solemn discussion with Nadim, a conversation concerning you and Sawyer."

Eden put down the second half of her sandwich, pushed the plate away from her. "You...you did?"

Ben picked up his napkin, dabbed at a small fleck of grape jelly that kissed the corner of Eden's mouth. Then he stood, took her hand in his, and led her out of the kitchen and to the couch in the family room.

"Ben?" she asked as she sat, as she looked up at him apprehensively. "Nadim is your enemy, isn't he? Haskim hinted—not that he would ever betray your confidence—but he did hint that your enemy was in your suite, not walking the streets of San Antonio."

"Haskim worries like an old woman," Ben said, joining her on the couch. "Nadim is not my enemy, not in the way you would believe. I am in no physical danger from him, Eden. But he is also an old man whose ambitions have been thwarted throughout his life. He is not above bringing me low in the eyes of our people to feel his life has been of some use."

She shook her head. "I don't understand, Ben. You're not worried Nadim might mount a coup, try to take over as sheikh?"

"Nadim might have hoped as much, many years ago, when my father was alive," Ben explained, taking her hand in his, stroking the soft skin on the back of her hand, her wrist. "This is why my father always kept him close, why I have kept Nadim close. But now he is old, his fangs no longer sharp, and his one hope to rule died when Leila—his daughter, my wife—died without bearing an heir to the throne. All Nadim can hope for now is to do mischief, as only young children and old men can.''

Eden covered Ben's hand with her own. ''And Nadim could make a considerable amount of mischief if he knew about Sawyer, about me, before you could find a way to tell your subjects about our existence?''

''He certainly would have tried,'' Ben agreed, ''which makes me doubly glad that I did not share with him, with anyone, my belief that I would come to Texas and find that you were the Eden Fortune of my heart.''

''He *would* have tried, Ben?'' she asked, shifting on the couch, looking at him carefully. ''He isn't going to try? Why? What did you do? Ben, you didn't do anything terrible, did you? He's an old man.''

''And Sawyer is my son,'' Ben said firmly. He stood and moved to stand in front of the fireplace, looking at Eden as he carefully chose his next words.

''Leila was Nadim's only child, and her memory is dear to him. I understand this, Nadim understands this. He knows what it is to protect his child, to want nothing but what is best for his child. And that is how I approached him, father to father."

"You asked him to help Sawyer because he's also a father, and would have to understand how you felt, how you'd want Sawyer protected from the sort of gossip, even condemnation, that could come once you'd acknowledged him? And Nadim agreed?"

Ben smiled, shook his head. "I should say yes now, Eden, and that would make you happy. But I cannot lie to you. If we are to have the future I would hope, we should never again lie to each other."

He picked up a photograph of Sawyer that sat on the mantel, smiled at it. "Everyone will love him. In time, even Nadim."

"Ben..." Eden persisted.

He replaced the photograph. "Leila died, as I have told you, but I have not told you how, or where," he began, then sighed. "She died in Rome, Eden, overcome by smoke in a rather small house fire." He looked at her levelly. "She died in bed, while sleeping in the arms of another man."

"Oh, Ben, I'm so sorry!"

"I am sorry for her death, the way of it, the how of it. But we did not love each other. I only wish she might have found happiness, but she had not. She had only met this man that same evening. Leila very much liked men, liked a variety of men."

He walked back over to the couch, took Eden's hands in his, pulled her to her feet. "Nadim came to me, nearly mad in his grief. He fell to the floor in front of me, begging that I help him hide the truth of Leila's death so that she might have the burial of a princess. So that her memory would live on, unsullied. I agreed, arrangements were made, and we never spoke of the matter again."

He was walking her toward the stairs, toward her bedroom, but now Eden halted, pulling at his hands. "And now you've blackmailed Nadim, haven't you? You've threatened to expose his poor dead daughter for what she was, to protect Sawyer?"

"No, Eden," he said quietly, leading her toward the stairs once more. "I would not do that to an old man, to Leila's memory. What I did was to remind him that happiness is to be grasped with both hands when the chance to hold it close is given to us. I reminded him of his love for his daughter, told him of my love for my son, and for my son's mother. And then I most respectfully asked for his help."

He could see Eden relax, see the worry lines fade from her forehead. "Then...then Sawyer will be all right? If...if you were to acknowledge him, if he were to go to...if he were to visit Kharmistan? He'd be all right?"

"If you were both to come to Kharmistan, you would both be, as you have said, *all right*," Ben told her, nuzzling her neck as, side by side, they moved up the staircase. "Nadim is, at the bottom of it, an honorable man."

Did Eden understand what he was saying to her? Did she believe him?

"But," he continued as they moved down the hallway, into the bedroom, "I would rather present my people with my son and my wife when I return to Kharmistan. Will I be able to do that, Eden? Will you marry me? Will you come home with me, bring Sawyer to his home?"

She stiffened under his hands, even as he was carefully lowering the zipper of her sundress. "I— I can't," she said, her hands still on his shoulders, her body with him, her mind fighting him every inch of the way. "I just can't."

"But you love me, Eden," he whispered against her ear, guiding them both to the bed, lying down beside her, looking deeply into her eyes. "Would you turn away from that love because you are fearful that Sawyer will not be happy in Kharmistan, with his father?"

Her bottom lip trembled as she raised a hand, stroked it down the side of his cheek. "I love you, Ben," she told him, her voice low, thick with emotion. "But you're asking me to jump blindly off a cliff, my son in my arms. How…how can I take him away from the only home he's ever known, his family—*my* family? Yours is a different world, a different culture...even a different language, different clothing, different foods..."

"I will promise to have both creamy and chunky peanut butter flown to the capital every month," he told her, trying to make a joke, knowing he had failed badly.

"Oh, God..." Eden buried her head against his chest, wrapped her arms tightly around him. "I need more time to think about all of this, Ben. I need to talk with my mother, my brothers. With Sawyer."

"I am not asking that you travel to the moon, Eden," Ben said, stroking her hair, removing the pins that held her warm curls so tightly confined. "We can visit often, and your family will always be welcome in our home. I cannot stay here, Eden, you have to know that. But how can you ask me to live without you, without Sawyer?"

Eden slowly turned onto her back, probably not even realizing that the bodice of her sundress now resided closer to her waist, that Ben was removing his own shirt so that he might be closer to her, feel her warm skin against his.

"I can't win, can I?" she asked quietly. "I can't ask Sawyer to give you up, now that he knows you exist. I can't rob him of his heritage, or his future. But at the same time, I will be asking him to give up so much here in Texas." She buried her head against his chest. ''Oh, Ben, why couldn't you have been a plumber from Dallas?''

He chuckled low in his throat as she held on to him, as he deftly removed the rest of their clothing.

He had told her what he'd done, how he had secured Nadim's cooperation. He had told her he loved her. He had asked her to be his wife. Now it was time to prove that he loved her, and he knew that the next minutes would be bittersweet. As he loved her. As he prepared to let her go.

He kissed her hair, her creamy throat. He murmured words of love to her in his own language, the language of poets who had written of love for centuries before most of the world had formed alphabets.

He loved her slowly, gently, replacing the needs and wants of last night with a languid loving that made silent promises he had every intention of keeping, if she would only allow them.

He worshiped her body, every creamy inch of it, with his hands, with his mouth. He brought her to climax once, twice, before even considering his own pleasure, his own release.

She was his, all his, as she melted beneath his touch, as she reformed into a living fire, as she held him, surrendered to him, made him a willing slave to the desire that fed them both, that lifted them, together, higher and higher.

She was silk, she was satin, she was the velvet night and the warmth of the sun. She was his food, his water, his reason for living, his only hope to ever feel alive.

He told her all of this in his native Arabic, soothing her with his words, setting new fires inside her most secret parts with his caressing fingers, his seeking tongue.

And then she became the aggressor. Without a word, she eased herself away from him, urged him onto his back as she leaned over him, her dark curls falling across her face as she looked at him, as her eyes spoke volumes no poet could ever successfully write.

She took, as he had taken. She gave, as he had given. Loving him, tracing her hands and lips along the length of his body, branding him hers forever.

If time could stop, if the world could grant them the gift of standing still, there would have been no shadow over their lovemaking.

And for a while, the world cooperated.

They came together at last, two halves of the same whole, the past remembered, the past forgiven and forgotten…the future too far away to be considered. Too far away to intrude, to hurt them with the reality that awaited them once the loving was over.

Eden cried out as Ben spilled himself inside her,

holding on to him tightly, saving him as he felt himself spinning, spinning out of control.

He held her in return as her body shuddered beneath him, cherishing her, protecting her, sheltering her from the almost agonizing pleasure that had gripped them both, tossed them about in an intense emotional storm like two small corks lost in a dark, velvety sea.

"He's leaving, Mom."

"Leaving? Why, Eden? When?"

"Tonight. He's saying goodbye to Sawyer now, and then he's leaving, going straight to the airport, to his private jet."

"And you're going to let him go?"

Eden turned away from the window, looked at her mother. "I can't ask him to stay. That would be impossible."

"And it would be just as impossible for you and Sawyer to go with him, share his life?" Mary Ellen asked, laying the needlepoint she'd been working on in her lap as she looked at her daughter. "Why? You belong together, darling, the three of you."

Eden turned to the window once more, watched as Ben and Sawyer walked away from the house, her son's small hand swallowed up in his father's larger one. "We've discussed it, Mom. We think it's best this way," she said, her heart breaking in her chest.

"You do? Really? How so, Eden? Please, explain this rational decision to your old mother, who fails to understand what you're talking about."

"And to your brother, who's equally in the dark," Holden said from the entrance to the living room before he walked over to kiss his mother. "I got here as soon as I could," he told her quietly, but not so quietly that Eden didn't overhear him.

"*Et tu, Brute?*" she asked him, trying to smile. "Thank you for coming, Holden, but this really is between Ben and me."

"And Sawyer," her brother pointed out reasonably. "Or are you going to tell me that you're doing this for Sawyer's own good?"

Eden rubbed a hand across her forehead, trying to fight off the headache that had gripped her as she struggled to control her emotions, tried so desperately not to cry. "Everything's just happening too fast, Holden. You can understand that, can't you? Mother?"

"My grandson is five years old and has just met his father," Mary Ellen answered, picking up her needlepoint once more. "I'd say things have been moving entirely too slowly, wouldn't you, Holden?"

Eden spread her hands, tried to make her mother

and brother understand. "Look— Ben's only known about Sawyer for a couple of days. I've only known the truth about Ben for a couple of days. We need to move slower, be more reasonable, consider how things should progress, *if* they should progress. Ben can go back to Kharmistan, speak with his advisors, begin to prepare his people for the reality of Sawyer's existence. I mean, there has to be some sort of protocol, doesn't there? Even a king can't just go to America, come back a week later, and say, 'Surprise! I have a son.'"

"And 'Surprise! I love that son's mother, and she's going to be your queen,'" Holden said, spreading his own arms wide. "Or hadn't you thought about that one, Eden? Being a queen, that is. Or a princess—whatever the heck you'd be as Ben's wife. Or is that what really scares you?"

She shifted her gaze to the floor. "Oh, I've thought about it, Holden," she admitted quietly. "And yes, the prospect scares me straight down to my toes."

"So you're both going to go slower," her brother said, nodding his head. "Ben goes back to Kharmistan, you go back to work, and Sawyer goes back to asking where in hell his daddy is. Sure. Right. Makes perfect sense. Dammit, Eden, none of us wants to see you go—but that's *nuts!*"

* * *

"You're going away, aren't you? You're going away, and you're never coming back."

"That is not true, Sawyer," Ben said, kneeling in front of his son. "I am going away, yes. That much is true. But I will be back. You are my son. I love you, Sawyer, and I will come to see you as often as I can. Just as I hope that one day soon your mother will see fit to allow you to come to Kharmistan, to visit me."

He ran his fingers through an unruly lock of Sawyer's dark hair, brushing it back off the small forehead, beating down an urge to pick his son up, to run with him as far and as fast as he could.

"Mommy won't let me go to see you, will she?" Sawyer asked, stepping away from Ben, kicking his booted toe into the soft dirt. "She wants me to stay here. Why? Tommy Barnes flies to California every summer to see his daddy. He flies in an airplane all by himself. Is Mommy afraid I'll get lost?"

This was hard, it was so hard. The hardest thing Ben had ever done. "Yes, Sawyer, I think maybe your mommy is afraid you might be lost. But she has promised to think about bringing you to Kharmistan later this summer, before you begin kindergarten."

"I'll go to school every day when I'm in kindergarten," Sawyer said, brightening a little. But then he frowned again, looking much older than his years, and much wiser, too. "Mommy always says *we'll see* when she really means no. That's what she said when I asked her if I could have Rollerblades. We'll see. And I never got them."

"She is your mother, Sawyer," Ben reminded the boy, "and you must trust her to know what is best for you. You do trust her, don't you?"

"I suppose so," the boy said, rubbing a finger under his nose. "My grandmother showed me on a map last night, showed me where Kharmistan is. It's pretty far away, isn't it? Are you sure you'll be able to find your way back here once you get home?"

"Not only will I find my way back here, Sawyer, but I will still phone you every night, just so that I can hear about your day and you can tell me about Hercules and Tommy Barnes and everything that makes you happy. And I will send you pictures of Kharmistan, of my home there. You would like to see pictures of my home, would you not?"

Sawyer nodded, not answering. He took Ben's hand in his and waited until Ben had regained his feet, then began leading him back to the house.

"We can take a picture of you, too, before you leave," he said, tugging harder on Ben's hand, seemingly eager to keep him moving. "My grandmother can take a picture of you and me and Mommy, and I can keep it in my room, and take it to school and everything. Okay?"

"That sounds like a fine idea," Ben told his son, then looked toward the front porch of the house, to where Eden was standing, watching them approach.

They were both being so sane, so sensible.

Did she feel as bad as he felt? Did she feel as if the bottom of her world had just fallen out, leaving her with nothing to hold on to, nothing to keep her upright?

Eden watched as Sawyer hugged his father good-bye, Ben kneeling on the front porch, his head buried against his son's neck. She pressed her hands to her mouth, holding back a sob as Sawyer, who had been so strong, burst into tears.

She was doing the right thing. They were doing the right thing.

Weren't they?

Mary Ellen hugged Ben, kissed his cheek, then took Sawyer's hand and led him into the house with the promise of some home-baked cookies and a large glass of milk.

Holden shook Ben's hand, clapped him on the back, mumbled something unintelligible, then followed his mother into the house. Leaving Eden and Ben alone on the porch, with Haskim discreetly inspecting the tires of the limousine.

"He will be all right," Ben said, taking Eden's

hand in his. "I have explained that I will phone him every day."

Eden nodded, then reached into the pocket of her blouse, extracting one of the instant photographs Holden had taken of the three of them earlier. "Here," she said, holding out the photograph, "you don't want to forget this."

Ben looked at the photograph, traced a finger over the three figures, then placed it in his pocket. "Well, I suppose it is time I was on my way. Nadim made it clear to me that we should be leaving for the airport before eleven and we must still return to the hotel."

"Ben," Eden began, then hesitated, cleared her suddenly tear-clogged throat. "I do love you. Thank you for understanding that, and for understanding that I need more time. I don't know if it would work out, living in Kharmistan. I—I wouldn't want Sawyer to settle in, just to discover that love isn't enough to bridge our two worlds. But I promise that I'll bring Sawyer to you soon. Maybe even next month. We'll visit, we'll talk, we'll see how Sawyer does…"

She wiped tears from her cheek, looked deeply into his eyes. "He's our son, Ben. We have to do what's best for him."

"I love him, too, Eden," Ben told her, stepping closer to her, taking her hands in his. "I love him, and you, enough to walk away, to keep Sawyer's identity our secret if you should decide that his life would be simpler if he were to remain here, never to claim his inheritance, his destiny. I love you both that much.''

''Oh, Ben,'' Eden said, sliding into his arms, closing her eyes as his strength enveloped her, perhaps for the last time.

Could their love survive another separation? Could Ben forgive her for her fears, her insecurities that kept her from believing that they truly had a future together, no matter how much they loved each other, would always love each other?

She held him, held on to him tightly, until at last he gently pushed her away, kissed her forehead, smiled into her eyes, said his last goodbye.

And then he was gone, and Eden stood on the front porch, watching the limousine driving away, hugging herself tightly as she fought to keep herself together, to keep herself from falling onto the porch and breaking into a million sobbing pieces....

Ben sat in one corner of the limousine, Nadim in the other, both of them silent as the driver cut through the night, heading toward the airport.

''I still do not understand, Your Highness,'' Nadim said at last, breaking the uncomfortable silence with an equally uncomfortable remark. ''To be a princess, to have her son as prince and future sheikh. What woman would deny herself this?''

Ben's smile was small, sad. ''A woman who loves her son, I suppose,'' he answered quietly, still looking out the side window, watching the dark Texas landscape. ''Not every woman craves power, Nadim, craves great wealth, a lofty position.''

He turned away from the window, looked at his chief advisor, whose bemused frown was almost comical. ''You have to admit one thing, Nadim. Eden could never be accused of taking advantage of me, of marrying me for anything other than love of your sheikh.''

Nadim's spine stiffened, even as he sat enveloped in his robes. ''You speak now of Leila?''

''No, Nadim, I do not, and forgive me if that is what you thought. Leila and I married for duty, which was acceptable to both of us at the time. Eden, however, was not raised to feel the responsibility of a princess marrying solely for the sake of the throne. As my son will not marry for the sake of his throne, when that day comes. I think, Nadim, we have all learned, much to our regret, the folly, and the pain, such unions often cause.''

''Yet you are confident Miss Eden Fortune will come to Kharmistan, to visit, to decide possibly to stay? That she will bring the prince with her?''

Ben unconsciously reached up, scratched at his

ear that was hidden beneath his white silk *kaffiyeh*. "Sawyer does not believe so."

"Then I do not understand, Your Highness. Why are we leaving?"

Ben reached into the pocket of his suit jacket, removed the photograph Eden had given him, passed it to Nadim. "Do you see her, my old friend? Look at her well, look into her eyes. Do you not see a woman of her word? Your king may not have his fairytale ending, but this is an honest, straightforward woman who will at least attempt to form some sort of compromise."

Nadim switched on a small overhead light, and looked at the photograph for a long time. "Yes, this is an honest woman. What I also see, Your Highness, is your son. There can be no question, Your Highness. This boy is your son, your heir. You and he are the future of Kharmistan, and I am its past."

He handed the photograph back to Ben, switched off the overhead light. "Once again, Your Highness, I thank you for your indulgence in allowing me to continue in the service of my prince. I may not have been so generous, were I in your place, knowing what I know about my own ambitions. This proves to me, at last, that you are the ruler Kharmistan needs, while I am nothing but a dreamer of lost dreams. I live to serve you, Your Highness, and to serve your son in any way possible."

"I will hold you to your promise, old friend, for Sawyer could only benefit from your teachings, as I have done."

"If he comes to Kharmistan," Nadim added dolefully. "If this honest woman allows him to claim his heritage… Ah, Your Highness, to place so much power in the hands of one woman. The future is here, as you say, with everyone open and honest and equal, but there is still much to say for the old ways."

Ben chuckled softly. "I had given some thought to throwing Eden over my shoulder and carrying her off to my palace. But I fought down the urge."

He sat forward, seeing the trailing runway lights ahead as the driver pulled onto the area of the airport reserved for private planes. He could see his own plane, a comfortably large white jet carrying the name of his homeland in flowing Arabic letters.

Lights were on inside the plane, the pilot visible in the cockpit, Ben's empty co-pilot chair waiting for him to occupy it. For once, the thrill of piloting the jet did not sweep through his system.

In mere minutes, they would be on their way.

"We are here, Nadim," he said, a tic beginning to work in the side of his jaw. "We are here, and soon we will be gone. Such a short visit to Texas, and so many changes in all our lives in that short time."

Haskim opened the door to the limousine, standing back as Ben stepped out, looked at the night sky, looked at the plane that would carry him away from Eden.

Was Sawyer right, and Eden would not come to him in Kharmistan?

Or was he right in having followed his heart, the heart he had given to Eden so many years ago, the heart he left with her now as he walked across a wet, glistening tarmac, toward the opened door of the jet....

Could he believe that leaving Eden was the best, most noble thing he could do? Could he believe that Eden would come to realize that he was not asking their son to give up his life, but offering him instead the dream of a new life that would be an extension of his previous life? A chance to experience all of his birthright, all of his potential as he grew into manhood?

Telling Eden he loved her, loved their son, enough to leave them had been hard, very hard. Now, walking slowly toward the plane, Ben almost found it impossible.

He had one foot on the bottom step, his hand on the railing, when he thought he heard Eden's voice.

His hand gripped the railing more tightly as he slowly turned, looked back across the inky tarmac.

Was he now doomed to hallucinations? To tricks played on him by his treacherous mind?

"Ben! Ben! Wait for us! We're coming with you!"

It was not a dream.

Eden was there, Sawyer beside her, and the two of them were running toward him, hand in hand, Sawyer gripping a small, battered teddy bear in his free arm. He could see them both clearly now, still running toward him across the tarmac, Eden's words now drowned out beneath the roar of the jet engines slowly coming to life.

"You are correct, Your Highness," Nadim said, standing beside him. "I have looked into her eyes and now I see for myself. This is an honest woman, who honestly loves you. The world is right once more."

Ben continued to stare at Eden. She was laughing, crying, and he knew that she had made her decision. He and Eden and Sawyer would be a family, forever and always, a family. She now believed what he believed, that as long as they were together, they were home.

Tears pricked at Ben's eyes, even as his smile threatened to split his face in two.

He let go of the railing, stripped off his *kaffiyeh*— not a sheikh at this moment, but only a man—and he began to run....

* * * * *

Here's a preview of next month's

*When a lone Texas lawman rescues
a bewitching lady who has lost her memory,
will he find himself lost in love?*

AN INNOCENT
WOMAN
by
Stella Bagwell

"**Y**our name is Gabrielle?"

His voice was low, rough and timbered with a Texas drawl. She resisted the urge to shiver. "Gabrielle Carter."

"Where are you from, Gabrielle?"

She swallowed as another wave of helpless fear swamped her. "I don't know."

His eyes, which seemed unusually light for such dark skin, narrowed with suspicion. "What do you mean, you don't know? Surely you know where you live?"

"I don't know," she repeated.

Sheriff Wyatt Grayhawk stepped closer and Gabrielle had to force herself to stand her ground and endure a closer scrutiny of his unnerving gaze. "Do you have any identification on you?"

Identification! She glanced down at her somewhat faded jeans, then quickly jammed her hands in all the pockets, searching for any scrap of paper. There was nothing. No coins or Kleenex or lipstick. Nothing.

She lifted shocked eyes back to his face. "No. I suppose my purse was in the car. Oh, God, and now it's burned!"

The young woman appeared to be genuinely distraught, Wyatt thought. But anyone would be after the jolt she must have taken when her car slammed into the oak tree. She was not a Texan. At first glance her appearance had told him that much, her voice had proved the notion even further. There was no wedding band or rings of any sort on her fingers. In fact, the only jewelry she was wearing were slender gold hoops in her ears.

"Is there anything left inside the car?" she asked hopefully.

"The metal is still too hot to search through the thing. I'll come back later and see what I can find. Unless you want to come clean right now?"

"Come clean? I'm sorry I don't know what you're talking about." She turned slightly toward him, her expression desperate. "Do you know who I am? If you do, why don't you tell me?"

Her voice was rising with each question as though she were very near to becoming hysterical. If she was faking this whole thing she was doing a damn good job, Wyatt thought. But hell, most women were good actresses. Lying to a man came as natural to them as breathing.

"Calm down, lady. If you've got a concussion it won't do you any good to get all excited."

Gabrielle's lips parted as she stared at him in stunned fascination. "Excited! How would you be if your head was cracking and you didn't know who you were or where you were? Oh, I'm sure a big strong man like you would take it all in stride," she sneered. "It would probably be just another day in the life of a Texas sheriff."

His nostrils flared as his eyes left the highway long enough to glance at her. "That ache in your head doesn't seem to be affecting your tongue."

She straightened her shoulders and lifted her chin. "I don't like being accused. And you were trying to accuse me of something!"

Except for a faint lift of his eyebrows, his features became deceptively passive. "If you do not know who you are, how can you be certain you aren't guilty?"

She opened her mouth to defend herself, but then a slow, sickening realization struck her. She might be a criminal. She might be anything. She just didn't know!

"You're right. I can't be certain of anything," she said wretchedly, then dropped her head in her hands.

Behind the wheel, Wyatt tried not to let the despair on her face soften him. She was a hell of a looker, but she could very well be up to no good.

In his work he had to be suspicious of everyone. And as a man there was no woman he trusted.

"You have no idea what you were doing on the road to the Double Crown Ranch?"

Gabrielle strained to remember, but all that would come to her mind was waking up with the floorboard of the car pressed against her face and the smell of gasoline choking her.

"No. The name means nothing to me."

"What about Fortune? Does that name register with you?"

She looked at him hopelessly. "If I've ever heard of it, I don't know it now. Who are these people? Could I have been going there to do a job?"

His lips thinned to a grim line. "That's what I'm wondering."

The sarcasm in his voice stung her. "What's that supposed to mean?"

"Nothing," he said bluntly. "We'll talk about it later. After you've seen a doctor."

That was fine with her. She was a little more than tired of his innuendos and vague accusations. The pain in her head was making her nauseous and thinking more than ten minutes into the future was terrifying. She simply wanted to close her eyes and forget the laconic sheriff beside her. She didn't want to be reminded of the fact that she knew nothing about Gabrielle Carter.

A few moments later his deep voice jerked her out of her jumbled thoughts.

"I wouldn't go to sleep if I were you."

She opened her eyes, but didn't bother to lift her head from the back of the seat. "Why?"

"If you've got a concussion you shouldn't sleep."

"I thought you were a sheriff. Are you a doctor, too?"

"No. Just a lawman."

Her gaze lingered on his rigid profile. "Grayhawk," she repeated. "Is that a Native American name?"

He didn't answer immediately. Finally he said, "My father was Cherokee."

"And your mother?"

"White. Like you."

Even through the haze of her pain, Gabrielle had picked up a sharp bitterness in his words. She wondered why, then just as quickly told herself it didn't matter to her if he hated white people or women, or even her. He was just one man in a big world. Once her memory returned, Sheriff Wyatt Grayhawk would be well and truly out of her life.

▼™ SILHOUETTE
SENSATION ®

AVAILABLE FROM 20TH APRIL 2001

I'LL BE SEEING YOU Beverly Bird

Kate Mulhern had never suspected that being a caterer was a dangerous occupation, but when your dinner client got murdered, it was! Thank heavens for rugged, sexy cops and twenty-four-hour protection!

ROGUE'S REFORM Marilyn Pappano

Ethan James had received a photo of a woman who, seven months ago, had claimed him body and soul—for a single night. A woman who was seven months pregnant...

IN A HEARTBEAT Carla Cassidy

Caleb McMann had wanted to meet the little girl whose life had been saved using his daughter's heart. He hadn't planned on falling for her and her beautiful mother while hiding his true identity!

HER SECRET GUARDIAN Sally Tyler Hayes

Soldier Sean Douglass had private reasons for coming by night to warn Dr Grace Evans of impending danger. But when she was kidnapped, he had to get up close and personal...

HEART OF MIDNIGHT Fiona Brand

Samantha Munroe was the only woman special agent Gray Lombard had ever loved and now she was in danger because of him. How could he protect her and what was the secret she was keeping?

A CERTAIN SLANT OF LIGHT Terese Ramin

What business did the suburban mum of four have falling for the dangerous, sexy undercover cop? What business did the tough, rugged cop have falling for the mum *and her kids* when he was on the job?

SILHOUETTE
DESIRE®

AVAILABLE FROM 20TH APRIL 2001

YOUR BABY OR MINE? Marie Ferrarella

Sexy single father Alec Beckett was very attracted to Marissa Rogers, his live-in nanny, also a single parent. Yet he'd sworn off female temptation. Now Marissa had to show him *exactly* what he was missing...

TALLCHIEF: THE HOMECOMING Cait London

Liam Tallchief pledged to reclaim his birthright for his young son's sake. And he didn't need any help from smart-mouthed Michelle Farrell. So why did he kiss her as if she were rightfully his?

SEDUCTION, COWBOY STYLE Anne Marie Winston

When Silver Jenssen came to town, Deck Stryker was fascinated to find out she was his enemy's sister. So he seduced her with mouth-watering caresses—until she discovered his betrayal and that she carried his child...

RIDE A WILD HEART Peggy Moreland

After their brief, turbulent affair, Carol Benson thought she'd seen the last of Pete Dugan. But here he was back in her life again and her body still craved his touch...

A ROYAL MARRIAGE Cara Colter

Royally Wed

Single mother Rachel Rockford needed a knight in shining armour...and Prince Damon Montague needed a wife. One marriage-of-convenience later, Damon had a princess bride he'd underestimated for she was determined to unlock his wary heart.

HER BABY'S FATHER Katherine Garbera

The Baby Bank

Journalist Reese Howard's instructions were to deliver one very fertile Sabrina MacFadden to the sperm bank and gather facts for his article. Under no circumstances was he to kiss Sabrina senseless, father her child, and force her to be his bride!

0401/22aa

SILHOUETTE
SPECIAL EDITION®

AVAILABLE FROM 20TH APRIL 2001

THE BABY QUILT Christine Flynn

That's My Baby!

When a sophisticated Chicago lawyer rescued Emily Miller and her baby no one would've expected anything to come of it. But the young mum and her newborn touched something in Justin Sloan…

MATT CALDWELL: TEXAS TYCOON Diana Palmer

He was rich, powerful and every woman's fantasy, but no woman had caught this sought-after bachelor's eye until his new employee roused his temper and his dormant desires.

THE MD SHE *HAD* TO MARRY Christine Rimmer

Conveniently Yours

All her adult life Lacey Bravo had loved Logan Severance, but the good doctor had never—well, just *once*—made an improper advance towards her. And the soon-to-be mum knew Logan would come after her demanding marriage…

THE SHEIKH'S KIDNAPPED BRIDE Susan Mallery

Desert Rogues

Swept away by the passionate Prince Khalil Khan, Dora Nelson revelled in her new fairy-tale life as Princess of El Bahar—until she discovered Khalil had lied to her…

SULLIVAN'S CHILD Gail Link

Years ago, blind ambition tore Rory Sullivan from Caitlyn Kildaire's tempestuous embrace, before she could tell him that he was about to become a father. But now he was back to take up where he had left off!

THE BRIDE SAID, 'I DID?' Cathy Gillen Thacker

The Lockhart Brides

Dani Lockhart had married her handsome enemy Beau Chamberlain…and couldn't remember doing it! She also didn't know how it was that she was expecting his child!

♦™ SILHOUETTE
INTRIGUE™

AVAILABLE FROM 20TH APRIL 2001

INTIMATE SECRETS BJ Daniels

An investigation into a jewellery theft brought Josie
O'Malley back into Clay Jackson's life. The woman he
never stopped loving had upped and left town two years
ago, and now it was apparent why. Who was the father of
her child?

RENEGADE HEART Gayle Wilson

Secret Warriors

Ex-CIA agent Drew Evans came to Maggie Cannon's
isolated home so he could enlist the young widow's help.
Only she and her daughter could prove his innocence.
Harbouring a fugitive put Maggie's life at risk, but the real
danger might be in falling in love with him…

INADMISSIBLE PASSION Ann Voss Peterson

Jackson Alcott was Brittany Gerritsen's prime suspect's
lawyer and the man who'd called off his engagement to
her. When someone tried to kill Brittany, it was Jackson
she turned to, Jackson whose steamy embraces and hot
kisses she never could resist…

THE SECOND SON Joanna Wayne

Lawman Lover

Honour-bound Sheriff Branson Randolph was just the
man Lacy Gilbraith needed right now. With someone out
to silence her, Branson took Lacy into protective custody.
But Lacy's real worry was losing her heart to the sexy
lawman!

0401/46aa